KILL THEORY

OTHER TEAM REAPER THRILLERS

Retribution

Deadly Intent

Termination Order

Blood Rush

Kill Count

Relentless

Lethal Tender

Empty Quiver

KILL THEORY

A TEAM REAPER THRILLER
BOOK 11

BRIAN DRAKE

BRENT TOWNS

ROUGH
EDGES
PRESS

Kill Theory
Paperback Edition
Copyright © 2025 (As Revised) Brian Drake

Based on characters by Brent Towns

Rough Edges Press
An Imprint of Wolfpack Publishing
1707 E. Diana Street
Tampa, FL 33610

roughedgespress.com

Paperback ISBN 978-1-68549-521-3
Ebook ISBN 978-1-68549-428-5

KILL THEORY

CHAPTER 1

Nogales, Mexico

A RED ROOF capped the brightly-lighted three-story hotel. The red roof and white walls served as a contrast against the clear blue sky and the desert, where cacti dotted the landscape for miles and rolling hills filled the background. It was a hostile environment, but if one were to turn the opposite direction from the one in which the non-descript four-door sedan traveled, one could experience the warmth and industriousness of Nogales without fear of ever dying of thirst next to a cactus.

"They're watching us," said the man in the back seat.

The driver glanced in the rearview mirror at the man in the passenger seat. He wasn't in a panic, but seemed close. The driver understood the nervousness; he felt a little, too, in the pit of his gut. But he was focused on their overall plan, a plan that would make them both very rich men.

Federico Esteves had to appease his passenger, the new president of Mexico. He passed the hotel without turning into the parking lot. The president's head rotated slowly as he tracked whatever had spooked him.

"What do you see, sir?"

The president sat forward. "They left their gunmen in the parking lot."

Esteves looked in the left side mirror, catching a view of the black cars and the at-post chauffeurs. The parking lot was empty. The cartel had bought out the entire hotel for the day specifically for their meeting.

The two luxury sedans near the entrance with the uniformed chauffeurs standing close was the sight that had upset the man in the back seat. Esteves saw why straight away. Bulges under the black driving jackets suggested heavy weaponry.

Federico Esteves, chief-of-staff to the new president of Mexico, headed for the next corner. He peeked in the rearview again. The other sight that had upset his passenger was across the street from the hotel, a small gathering of Nogales citizens who knew something wasn't quite what it should be; that a cartel presence at the hotel would occupy gossip for the next week.

Esteves said, "What do you want to do, sir?"

The man in the back seat sighed audibly. "I will have to wear the disguise."

Esteves cracked a grin. "Yes, sir."

He drove until he found a church with an empty parking lot. He pulled into a space and passed back a suitcase. The man in the back seat opened the case.

He watched in the rearview while the white-haired man donned a black wig and pulled it down over his graying but full head of hair, checking in a hand-held mirror to make sure none of his true hair showed. He behaved as if this process was perfectly natural, and not at all ridiculous. Lastly, the man put on a pair of wide-framed glasses.

"Should be good enough," Esteves said.

"I don't want good enough."

"They've only seen you on TV or in the newspapers," Esteves said. "There's no way they'd believe their newly-elected president was walking into a small hotel in Nogales to meet with two cartel leaders."

The man in the back seat said, "I told them no weapons, nothing out of the ordinary."

"The way it is, Mister President."

Mexican President Lucio Rojo bit off a curse.

Esteves left the church parking lot and returned to the hotel. As they pulled in, the gathered crowd started to run away.

"Why are they running?" President Rojo asked.

"They might think you're a cartel kingpin. Why else have armed troops out front?"

"I'm beginning to regret this course of action," the president said.

Esteves said nothing more. The endless discussions leading up to this day had annoyed him no end. Rojo had a plan for peace in Mexico. That plan required a number of sacrifices. Esteves thought the sacrifices were worth the cost, the amount of which was unknown at present, but anything they could do to stop drug violence was okay with him. Even if the effort ultimately filled his pockets. That was a bonus. A big bonus.

He stopped the car beside the other two sedans and gave his boss a last glance in the rearview.

"Are you ready?"

Rojo nodded. "Yes."

Esteves left the air-conditioned car for the hot outside. He nodded to the chauffeurs, who did not move as he opened the back door to let his president step into the heat.

Lucio Rojo, looking quite ridiculous with his wig and glasses, buttoned his suit jacket. He stood with his shoulders back, as dignified as he could muster. He handed the briefcase that had contained his disguise to Esteves, who carried it in his right hand.

Rojo was taller than the slightly-built Esteves, normally with a full head of white hair and character lines on his face that testified to rough living. He looked quite proper in his black suit, but there had been a time when he'd had no access to such fine clothing.

Rojo and Esteves did not have security of their own. Esteves, per Rojo's instructions, wasn't armed. Rojo had no reason to fear the cartel leaders. They were forming an alliance. Making new arrangements. Arrangements beneficial to both sides. Which made Esteves wonder why Rojo was so nervous. During the campaign, he hadn't shown a moment of reconsideration.

But then, it had all been talk. Now he actually had to implement the plan.

Esteves agreed with one thing, though. Posting armed troops outside was an insult.

He knew better than to say so to men who could snuff him out with as much emotion as turning off a light switch, however.

It wasn't hard to find where the other cartel bosses waited once Rojo and Esteves entered the quiet building. Two bodyguards in dark suits stood outside a conference room, and Esteves approached them. The bodyguards did not insult the government officials with a pat down.

They'd at least provided *that* courtesy.

Esteves entered the conference room with the Mexican president behind him. It was small, the carpet a dark brown and the walls covered in a light-colored wood paneling. The table was solid oak. Very rustic, bright, and clean. One wall was actually three panes of glass that looked in on an office center—copy machines and computers, all unoccupied.

Two men sat at the table. Bottles of water had been placed nearby.

Esteves pulled out a chair for Rojo, who sat, and then he took the chair beside his boss. He placed the briefcase on the floor beside his chair. Esteves regarded the other two faces curiously. Neither man was smiling. Their dark eyes regarded him with something less than friendliness.

"We're glad you could make it, Mister President; Mister Esteves," said the man immediately to his right.

Victor Zamorano ran the northern branch of the cartel named after him, with a 30-million-peso price on his head. His face looked like a rock, with chips and crevices, and his age wasn't helping. He might have looked rugged and handsome in his younger days, but as gravity took over, he looked less and less like a pinup model and more like an old man.

"You sound like you weren't sure we'd be here," Esteves said. "Even though we asked for this meeting?"

"We weren't," said the other cartel boss.

Chucho Banderas glared at Esteves while twisting the cap off a bottle of water. He passed it to Esteves.

"You look a little thirsty."

Esteves took the bottle and handed it to Rojo. Rojo shook his head and Esteves placed the bottle on the table.

The cartel bosses laughed.

Banderas was the top torpedo with the Plancante Cartel, which not only covered another part of northern Mexico that Zamorano didn't, but also parts of the U.S. It was a quick trip over the border into Arizona or New Mexico from Nogales. Banderas's men made many such trips. A new drug processing station on the New Mexico side allowed them to move more raw materials into the States than if they'd processed the drugs on the Mexico side, which meant a larger supply for U.S. customers once the processing plant worked its magic.

"I don't understand this antagonism," President Rojo said. "And I said no guns. Why are there two men out front with guns? If anybody is paying attention to this building after we finish here, our work will be for nothing."

"You don't tell us what to do," Zamorano said. He laughed again. Banderas laughed too.

"What is so funny?"

"What's with the wig?" Zamorano said.

Rojo glared at the two men as he removed the glasses and angrily pulled off the wig. Esteves had his hand out for both items and Rojo took advantage of the offered hand. Esteves put both items in the pockets of his suit jacket.

The cartel leaders still grinned.

Rojo took a deep breath. Cartel leaders were always difficult to deal with. He figured this pair were purposefully trying his patience, because they wanted to see if what he'd been saying on the campaign trail, and in private, was going to be backed up with action.

"I asked for this meeting to make a gesture of good faith, and propose a change in Mexico policy that will benefit both of us."

Banderas said, "Our spies have told us what you have in mind. Forgive us if we don't believe you."

"Start talking," Zamorano added.

CHAPTER 2

ROJO SMILED as he regarded the two men across the table. They were masters of their craft, if one could refer to the manufacturing of deadly narcotics as a craft. They were responsible for countless murders and kidnappings. Millions of addicts around the world who committed minor crimes to buy more of their drugs. And if they weren't directly involved, they gave the orders to the men who carried out the violence and sold the product. They were not good people. Zamorano, Rojo knew, was devoted to his daughter, a 6-year-old named Annabelle, and while he understood that murderers could also be good fathers, it didn't put his nerves at ease. Zamorano could order his death as casually as ordering a Cuban sandwich.

And he'd heard doubts such as those expressed by the equally ruthless Banderas many times. The only way to show somebody that you meant business was to take action instead of playing chin music.

Rojo meant business, but he was also a politician,

and such characters were known for more talk and less action. Lucio Rojo wanted to break the mold.

Rojo hadn't always aspired to political power. Growing up near Cabo San Lucas, he'd worked with his father at various tourism-related businesses, but taking money from gringos, while delighting his father and providing for him a good education, did not represent how Rojo wanted to spend the rest of his life.

He graduated college with an engineering degree and quickly found employment with the government, focusing on infrastructure matters. The job opened his eyes to the plight of his fellow Mexicans who did not benefit from the lush funds available in Cabo, which, to Rojo, was an entirely different country from the one his fellow citizens resided within. Poverty, homelessness, crumbling roads, all of the miseries that took away from the quality of life hard-working people deserved became front and center. He couldn't simply sit in an office while he knew others, some more deserving than he, were struggling.

Rojo joined the Institutional Revolutionary Party in the early 2000s, rising in prominence and winning several local elections and eventually the governorship of his home state of Tebasco. From there, at the end of his second term, he launched his presidential campaign.

He fought hard, and won against opponents who were as eager to steer Mexico on the path to prosperity as he.

Rojo claimed that prosperity was impossible with drug violence so prominent, and, virtually, out of control.

Hence the meeting with the cartel leaders.

Zamorano and Banderas waited patiently for him to

begin, and he took a deep breath before uttering the first words.

"The drug war has to end," Rojo said.

Low laughs from the cartel leaders.

"What do you mean?" Zamorano said.

"The violence is out of hand on both sides, Mister Zamorano. All we do is kill each other."

"And we've paid off so many people in your government," Banderas said, "that we get our product through no matter how the army and police try to stop us. What does this *ending* look like to you?"

"It would be nice if we could call a truce."

Zamorano and Banders laughed again.

"A truce?" Zamorano said.

"I am willing to stop police and military persecution of the cartels."

"In exchange for what?" Zamorano said.

"I want the payoff money to continue."

More laughs from the cartel leaders.

"The cartels," Rojo continued, ignoring the laughter, "will in turn no longer shoot policemen, ambush the military, or engage in the kidnapping and murder of citizens to send threats of compliance. You will not fight amongst yourselves. In exchange, you will be allowed to continue business."

"This is madness," Zamorano said.

"Why?"

"Nobody is going to believe this," the cartel leader said. "Other nations—especially the United States—are going to interfere. How much money and support have they given Mexico to support the drug war?"

"A lot."

"And they aren't going to see that money go down

the drain. Have you thought about what you are going to tell them?"

Rojo said nothing.

"Have you thought about our associates now sitting in this country's jails awaiting extradition to the United States?" Zamorano said. "What are you going to do with them?"

"What is done is done," Rojo said. "Your associates will not be let out. That's one way we plan to placate the Americans. They can have their prisoners for their expensive trials and convince themselves that their time and money has been worth the effort."

"Or," Banderas said, "those prisoners can be returned to their homes. You claim to want to help the Mexican people, right? Are those people not Mexicans?"

Rojo swallowed. He had expected hardball, and he was getting it in spades.

The president knew there was only one way to end the chuckles and the conflict.

He had to admit to them that he had help.

From Americans in the heart of the U.S. government.

CHAPTER 3

"WHY DOES the United States matter to us?" Chucho Banderas, leader of the Plancante Cartel, said. "What are they going to do? Send the Marines to invade?" He laughed.

"We have help," Rojo said.

Esteves grumbled beside him. Rojo shook his head, but didn't take his eyes off the cartel leaders.

"What kind of help?" Zamorano said.

"From the Americans."

"Mister President—"

Rojo shushed Esteves.

Zamorano and Banderas exchanged looks. Zamorano faced Rojo.

"That changes things."

"I thought it might."

"Who are these Americans?"

"You don't need to know their names."

"Are they even real?" Banderas said.

"They're real, and they're in the upper echelon. I am not the only one," Rojo said, "who thinks the violence needs to stop. Business, however, does *not* need to stop. It is none of our concern what people, of their own free will, decide to put into their bodies. Why should we risk lives to prevent that? How much more are we willing to lose?"

Zamorano blinked.

"Both sides have lost heavily," Rojo said. He sensed he had them on the ropes. Now was the time to go for the final punch. He continued, "How much more are *you* willing to lose?"

Zamorano and Banderas remained stone faced, but Rojo didn't want to press further. He had them on the hook. Esteves, to Rojo's right, shifted uncomfortably. Rojo knew his chief of staff hadn't wanted to reveal the fact that they had American support, but there was no other way. Rojo needed the cartels on board. He had promised his voters peace. The only way to achieve peace was to literally make a deal with the cartel devils, he understood that, and was willing to take the risk. Zamorano and Banderas were the two devils that carried influence over the other cartels across the nation, big and small; the independents, too. If these two cartel leaders jumped aboard the plan, the other cartels would fall in line, especially once they realized the mutual benefit.

"This idea is too good to be true," Chucho Banderas said.

"What can I do?" Rojo said. "What do you need?"

"Certain reassurances," Zamorano said.

"Such as?"

"We need some bodies stacked in a field to make sure you and your American friends are not playing us for fools," Zamorano said. "I promise, if this is some sort of trick, our vengeance will shock even the coldest of hearts, Mister President."

"You want to ambush an army unit?"

"No," Zamorano said. "We want to wipe out one group in particular, one group of American fighters that have been a thorn in our side for many years."

"Team Reaper," Banderas said. "You bring us the heads of Team Reaper, and we'll agree to your proposal."

Rojo smiled. "Wouldn't it be better," he said, "if your people *collected* the heads of Team Reaper?"

"And how do you suggest we go about doing that?" Zamorano said.

Rojo turned to Esteves. The chief of staff grabbed the briefcase from the floor and snapped the locks. Lifting the lid, he passed a thick folder to the president.

Rojo placed the file in the center of the table. The cartel leaders' eyes snapped to the folder.

"This file contains pertinent information on John Kane and his colleagues," Rojo said. "As a bonus, I can even tell you where Team Reaper is, at this moment."

"Where?"

"Here in Mexico. Southern region. They are working with agents of our federal task force."

The men around the table fell silent.

Rojo said, "Perhaps you can think of a way to send the Americans a Valentine, considering it *is* February and the holiday only a week away?"

Zamorano grinned. "Some fresh red roses, maybe?"

"The redder," Rojo said, "the better."

Presently the meeting ended. Rojo and Esteves left first, but not before Rojo once again donned his ridiculous disguise.

He didn't want to take any chances of being seen, but nobody outside the hotel took notice of their departure.

Esteves said, "No turning back now, sir."

"There was never a question of not doing this, Federico," Rojo said. "I promised voters peace. We *will* have peace in Mexico."

One way or another.

To Rojo, the United States had never done Mexico any favors and had, in fact, treated them as second-class bumpkins when it came to the drug war.

He saw no reason to grant them special treatment.

CHAPTER 4

Otero County, New Mexico, South of Alamogordo

IT WAS SUPPOSED to have been a romantic camp out far from civilization.

That's how it started, anyway, with newlyweds Gus and Monica Alfred driving their old-school Jeep south on Highway 59, away from Alamogordo, away from Hollman Air Force Base, past White Sands, deep into the desert where only majestic scenery awaited them, and they were the only humans for miles.

They weren't on an official camp ground. It was the literal middle of nowhere where they pitched their tent and set up a camping stove and dug a pit for a fire. The daytime sun shined bright, the sky a clear blue, and green-and-tan mountains the only thing they wanted to see other than each other. The ground was hard-packed and dry, unforgiving, but they were away from the hustle and bustle, enjoying peace and quiet, with only assorted desert critters showing their presence, but also keeping their distance.

And, in case of trouble from said critters, Gus Alfred had packed a semi-auto Benelli shotgun loaded with double-aught buck and a six-pack of slug loads strapped to the shoulder stock. Monica was no slouch in the gun department, either. She packed a Ruger .357 in her purse, the six-shooter stoked with semi-jacketed hollow-points.

They sat side by side on loungers, the fire burning in front of them, the desert beyond extra dark from the glare of the flames. They might as well have been sitting in the deepest region of space.

Gus was an entrepreneur who ran a trio of automotive parts stores throughout New Mexico; Monica worked as a city attorney for Alamogordo, specializing in civil matters.

"Do you hear that?" Gus said, rising from the lounger.

Monica heard the noise, too. "Sounds like a truck."

"Diesel motor. Maybe other campers?"

"At this time of night?"

Monica was no fool. Her father, a career police officer in Arizona, had instilled in his daughter a sense of hypervigilance. She left the lounger and went to the Jeep, grabbing her revolver from the purse on the floor and calling for Gus to get his shotgun.

Gus approached the car. "I don't think—"

Headlamps hit them like a concert spotlight.

The big Ford truck had crested a hill and, rolling over the top, stopped with the bright lights shining on the camp site. The truck remained still, the diesel humming, as the couple stepped behind the Jeep for cover.

"What are they doing?" Monica said.

"Surprised as we are," Gus told her. He was taller than his wife. She looked small beside him as they waited behind the Jeep.

The truck started forward again, slowly, turning to give the camp site a wide berth until it was even with the driver's side of the Jeep. The truck stopped again. The engine chugged. Gus and Monica stayed low on the passenger side of the Jeep. Gus was shaking. He took a deep breath. He didn't want Monica to see him nervous. He ignored standard gun safety protocols and kept his finger on the trigger. He heard the hammer on Monica's revolver click back. She had the same feeling as he.

The truck's driver's side window powered down. The driver's face wasn't visible, but the glow from the fire was enough to highlight the dark snout of a double-barreled shotgun.

Gus shouted, "Down!" and shoved Monica into the dirt with his left hand while firing the Benelli twice in rapid succession. He joined her on the ground as the Double-O buckshot slammed into the truck's metal.

Doors opened and slammed. Monica scooted to the rear bumper while Gus moved to the front, shouldering the Benelli. Neither he nor Monica was a combat veteran, but both trained regularly with firearms, participating bi-annually in three-gun competitions throughout the state. He knew how to shoot targets under the pressure of a timer, but live targets were something he'd only imagined, never truly anticipating engagement of any kind. Monica only knew about shooting two-legged threats from stories her father told.

His throat was dry, his vision already constricting, his pulse racing. He had more to protect than himself.

The two burly men emerging from the truck wore dark-clothes. Their facial features still eluded him as the flickering firelight competed with the desert darkness.

The one with the shotgun raised his weapon at the rear of the Jeep, where Monica hid. Gus tightened his finger on the Benelli's trigger once again. The shotgun bucked as the other shotgunner fired. Gus's pattern struck, splitting open the shotgunner's left arm and part of his chest. He yelled and fell, his partner spinning Gus's way with a short submachine gun at his hip. Flame flashed from the automatic weapon. Gus was suddenly on his back, pain spreading through his legs and belly. Monica's revolver cracked sharply, but another burst from the automatic weapon ended the bark of single-shots.

Gus heard footsteps approaching, boots crunching on the hard ground, but he still couldn't see. It was getting darker by the second, and eventually Gus saw nothing more whatsoever.

———

Miquel Esperanzo knelt beside the male. There was no need for another burst. The string of .380 slugs from his Ingram M-11 had done their job. He already knew the woman was dead.

He hustled back to his fallen compatriot, who

wailed on the desert floor. Agony etched Jorge Corza-on's face.

The two men communicated in a flurry of Spanish, Jorge pleading with Miquel not to leave him there. Miquel had no intention of doing that. He and Jorge had grown up together in the same rat-invested neighborhood. Their bond was tighter than blood. But Miquel had to admit that there was nothing he could do about the wounds except general first aid. He left the Ingram on the ground and grabbed Jorge under each arm, dragging him the distance from the Jeep to the Ford truck. Jorge screamed and passed out.

Miquel grunted and strained as he boosted Jorge into the back seat of the truck. Jorge was not a light man, and the blood leaking from the shotgun wounds soaked Miquel's clothes. Their drive north from south of the border was supposed to be uneventful. The new smuggling route had been scouted time and time again; there was nothing and nobody within miles. Why had these campers been in the area?

Miquel secured Jorge and shut the back door. He leaned against the cab, gasping. The covered truck bed was undamaged, which meant the contraband under-neath was undamaged. Miquel scooted behind the wheel and put the truck in gear once again. He continued on the drive.

The plan had to change. He couldn't let Jorge bleed out in the back seat. Miquel had to reach Alamogordo via 59 and fast. He knew of an off-the-books doctor used by the cartel that he could bring Jorge to. From there he'd contact the processing plant and let them know the delivery was going to be late.

The late hour might help him avoid unwanted

attention. The truck had pellet damage from the shotgun blast. Somebody was bleeding in the back seat. Miquel would have to mind the speed limit, and keep the A/C on to keep from sweating profusely.

It was going to be a long night.

CHAPTER 5

MIQUEL ESPERANZO'S memorized instructions regarding the medical contact in Alamogordo stated he reach the clinic, park, and call the doctor. It was a 24-hour clinic in the middle of a shopping complex, so the truck blended in. A big blue lighted sign above the front door stating the clinic's purpose. Miquel ignored Jorge's increased cries of pain as he quickly dialed. It wasn't the clinic's number, but a private line. Somebody's cell.

"Yes?"

If the doctor didn't hear Jorge wail as Miquel began talking, he had to be deaf. Miquel Esperanzo communicated the need and the doctor told him to bring his car around to the back. He would meet them there. Miquel swung the truck around to the rear door, which was already cracked open. A white man in scrubs with blond hair stepped out.

Miquel powered down his window.

"Where is he?"

"Back."

The doctor looked, nodded, said: "I'll get a

stretcher. We're going to put him in a back room and take care of him, all right?"

"Fine, fine. Hurry."

The doctor hurried back inside and returned with a black assistant and a stretcher. Miquel Esperanzo jumped out and opened the rear door and let the medics do their work. The blond doctor made a partial examination of the bullet damage, said something his assistant agreed with, and the two of them hefted the bleeding Jorge Corzaon onto the stretcher.

Miquel watched them wheel his friend inside. Was the whole clinic on the take? Anything was possible when the cartel threw money around like confetti. Miquel looked around quickly. It was late, the other storefronts, though lighted in some cases, displayed only Closed signs. A few stray cars littered the parking lot.

He held the back door open while the medics wheeled Jorge into the building. He watched them wheel him into an exam room. He couldn't join them yet.

He let go of the door and grabbed a cell phone from his pocket. He had to report what had happened. The delivery would be delayed while the medics took care of Jorge. Miquel could not complete the delivery himself. He needed his friend, and his friend's gun. The chances of a hijacking were too great. The cartel would understand.

A little.

———

"Who found the camp site?" asked the sheriff.

"A chopper pilot from the air base flew over the area and called it in," said the deputy.

Otero County Sheriff Vartan "Vic" Nazarian wondered how they'd have learned of the murders otherwise. Who would want to camp in the desert rather than any of the many state-operated campgrounds in the area?

Well, he had an idea why. Even state parks could get crowded, and also expensive, and sometimes not worth the cost and effort it took to find a spot where some dumb Bubba wasn't making a racket all night. If you wanted to be alone in this day and age, you had to go to extremes.

Nazarian and Deputy Keely Lynton left the Bronco at the perimeter of the camp site, now a homicide site, and approached carefully. In appearance, they were polar opposites. He was pushing six-five, broad in the chest, thick at the arms and legs, his rock-like face reflecting years of hard living and rough experience.

Keely Lynton, shorter than her boss, was a California transplant. Having grown up in the leisurely world of Orange County, she had fled her home to find "real life", as she put it, and her search led her to New Mexico. She could not, however, shake the girl-next-door look, her blonde hair a striking feature, along with the freckles dotting her cheeks.

The crime scene crew, supervised by another deputy named Hayes, didn't look up from their work. The stench was terrible; the buzzing flies ignored. The sheriff and Lynton went to Hayes.

"What's the score?" Nazarian asked.

Hayes scratched his graying goatee. "Couple of campers murdered."

"Gun fight?"

"They did some shooting. Shotgun shells on the ground there, the woman's revolver was empty."

"Did they hit anything?"

"Blood spatter over there," Hayes pointed to a spot on the ground. Nazarian followed the deputy's finger. The blood puddle was behind the yellow line, but still obvious in contrast with the desert dirt.

Deputy Keely Lynton said, "Looks like tire tracks."

"From a truck, mostly likely," Hayes said. "I've already measured the tread and sent the info to HQ. The tracks are deeper over by the hill, where it looks like the tires sunk deeper when the truck braked hard."

Nazarian offered no reply as he examined the camp site quietly. His hat protected him from the sun's glare, his dark skin making him stand out the most between his two deputies, Keely Lynton's pale skin especially.

The fire pit had gone out long ago. The couple had died near the Jeep, as if in defensive positions. He'd certainly been in enough gun fights to know how to use a vehicle for cover, and this pair was no different.

They'd brought weapons to protect themselves from four-legged threats, and ran into human predators instead, except the two-legged predators had the ability to shoot back.

Nazarian already had an idea how the scene played out.

"The couple was enjoying the night, and the truck showed up."

"Right," Hayes said.

"Who was in the truck?"

"Who do you think?" Keely Lynton said. "What's the chatter stream been saying the last six months?"

Nazarian ignored the question. "The crew in the truck wasn't expecting anybody to be here, so they stopped. The gun fight happened, and the couple was good enough to hit one of them."

"But they didn't win the fight," Lynton said.

"Yeah," the sheriff said. "But we have blood. We have tire treads. And if the wounded man was hit with the shotgun, he's not going to simply walk it off."

"What do you want us to do, Sheriff?" Hayes said.

"The wounded man will need medical attention. We need to hit the small clinics in the area, especially the usual suspects who we know assist cartel operatives."

"Unless we find another body up the highway," Lynton said.

"We might. See any buzzards flying around?"

Deputy Lynton admitted she did not.

Nazarian told Hayes and Lynton to drive back to headquarters together while he drove back alone. He made a phone call along the way to a friend at Homeland Security and asked for a late lunch meeting.

His friend agreed.

Nazarian drove with his mind occupied by one thought, the answer to Deputy Lynton's question about the "chatter stream" of late.

And that's what he wanted to talk to his friend from Homeland Security about.

CHAPTER 6

THE WAITRESS SEEMED OVERLY happy but Vic Nazarian and his friend from Homeland Security smiled back as she put plates in front of them and departed with a pop of her bubble gum.

Nazarian looked at Peter Lewis as he salted his fries. The representative from Homeland hadn't said much since they met at the diner. They were both dealing with heavy workloads that never lifted. It was a repeat of a process Vic Nazarian had seen since his days as an Army Ranger and later a rookie cop. You join the police to do something challenging, that only a few people can do; you want to do something good, protect people, serve the public, bust bad guys.

You end up maintaining a status quo where crime never stops, prisons have a revolving door, and the best you can hope for is to hold back as much of the violent tide as possible.

Like now.

But Nazarian had an idea...

"Did you hear about the homicides in the desert?"

Lewis chewed and swallowed a mouthful of hamburger. "Came across my desk, yeah. Why?"

"Two civilians ambushed by drug runners, is what we think."

"You sure?"

"The couple had weapons. They shot back. We saw plenty of shell casings. It got hot there, Pete. I don't know who those civilians were, but they didn't take it lying down."

"Good for them."

"They're still dead. And we have at least two drug runners on the move."

"They hit anybody with all those shots?" Lewis said. He ate a French fry. He was getting thicker in the middle from riding a desk instead of a patrol car like in his younger days, but he still had a full head of hair and had recently grown a thick dark mustache.

"We think so. At least one."

"Go find the guy. We know most of the off-books doctors who help the cartel, right?"

"That's not the point, Peter."

"What *is* the point, Vic? What do you expect the federal government to do?"

"Secure the border, for one thing."

"In progress."

"Not fast enough."

"I'm not in charge, Vic. Call your senator."

Nazarian sighed and finally started eating. He didn't want his own burger to get cold. Out the window beside them, beyond the parking lot, lay brown desert stretching to infinity, and tall mountains seemingly unable to contain the vast open space. An otherwise peaceful setting. But there was truly nothing peaceful about the environment overall.

"Why are the check points closed?" Nazarian said.

"Well—"

"Don't bullshit me, Peter."

"Don't worry."

"I *do* worry. There are innocent people in harm's way."

"Look, I get it. We're as upset about that as you are. There is so much activity at the California and Arizona border that we had to move people from New Mexico to help handle the load."

"And left New Mexico vulnerable in the process? Because the illegals aren't crossing here?"

"Well—"

"It's happening here, too, Pete. The cartels are taking advantage of the gap, and people in my county are suffering. Some of them are *dying*. Like the couple last night."

The man from Homeland said nothing. He dropped his eyes to his plate of food.

Nazarian frowned as he chewed another bite. There was something his friend wasn't telling him. He pressed a little harder.

"We need those checkpoints. What's the real problem?"

Peter Lewis sighed. He suddenly appeared as if an invisible weight had landed on his shoulders.

Nazarian didn't like that look at all.

"The border check points aren't simply *closed*, Vic."

"What do you mean?"

"You can't tell anybody about this. *Nobody*."

"I won't."

"They've been defunded."

Nazarian flinched. *That's not what I expected.* "Defunded. Really?"

"It's temporary."

"I'm not stupid, Pete. It will take an act of Congress to re-fund the check points now. How long does the federal government plan to leave New Mexico in the lurch?"

"I don't know."

"You don't *know*?"

"I'm as frustrated as you, Vic."

"It won't be long before the illegals and terrorists take advantage too."

"No, it won't," Lewis said. He ate some more. His appetite apparently wasn't affected by the situation, but Vic Nazarian knew the real story. They saw and dealt with so much crap, from the government to the lawbreakers, that they couldn't let it affect their own health.

"My county," Nazarian said, "is seeing an increase in drug activity and drug-related murder. Never mind individuals committing crimes to get a fix. We're facing a crisis here, Pete."

"I know."

"Being mad isn't going to get us anywhere."

"True."

"I have to protect my county."

"You do. No argument there."

Nazarian and Lewis ate a while. The sheriff didn't mind letting the silence linger. He had a bomb to drop on the Homeland representative.

"Did you ever hear about the Armenian Genocide, Pete?"

"I know *about* it. Nothing more than what's said in public now and then."

"That's nothing compared to what really happened, but we don't have time to go into that. My family were victims of that genocide. Some of them, anyway. The ones that survived took the fight back to the Turks. Ever hear of Operation Nemesis?"

"No."

"Armenian revenge for the slaughter. No prisoners, Pete. We killed everybody in front of us. We especially targeted those responsible."

Peter Lewis nodded.

"Perhaps a modern version of that kind of justice needs to be revived in the United States."

"That's insane."

"The right people can make it happen."

"The right people will end up in *prison*, too, Vic. Is that where you want to go? Is that going to be your legacy as sheriff of this county?"

"My legacy, so far, will be that of the sheriff who couldn't keep safe the citizens the people elected him to protect. I don't intend to be that guy, Pete."

"The answer isn't a death squad."

"Then what is?"

"I don't know."

Nazarian ate some more as frustration flowed through him. Lewis finished his hamburger and nibbled at another fry or two before pushing his plate away.

"Not hungry anymore?" Nazarian said.

Lewis snapped a glare at Nazarian before looking out the window. "I can't support what you're suggesting."

"I know."

"But that's only officially."

"Uh-huh."

"What do you have in mind?"

"You assume I have a plan already?"

Lewis looked back at Nazarian. "We've known each other since college, Vic. You never talk about anything, not something big like this, without already having a plan at least worked out in your head."

Nazarian only smiled. It wasn't a happy smile, though. It was the smile of a man who knew the next choices he made might result in not only his death, but the deaths of others; a man who had to make up his mind that such an ending was okay as long as his death achieved the desired results.

He wasn't sure Peter Lewis would understand.

CHAPTER 7

Southern Mexico

"THREE BOGIES ON YOUR TAIL, Reaper One," said Cara Billings over the com unit.

"We're running as fast as we can! Can you take them out?"

"You're in the way. Break right."

John "Reaper" Kane didn't need Cara Billings to repeat the suggestion. He turned sharply to the right, his boots kicking up a cloud of dust as his two teammates followed.

"Down!" Kane shouted.

Kane, Axe Burton, and Carlos Arenas dived behind a cluster of cacti. The ground beneath them was hard-packed and hot, unforgiving terrain.

But it was where the enemy lived, so that's where they had to go.

"Incoming," said Cara.

Kane, Axe, and Arenas stayed low. The cracks of Cara's sniper rifle, somewhere in the rocky hills behind them, echoed across the desert landscape, two shots total, the whip-crack of the passing projectiles a welcome sound.

The three cartel gunners chasing Kane and his teammates didn't react in time. Their attention was on pursuit of the three men running from them; they never thought they'd run straight into one of the best snipers Kane had ever known.

The last man in the trio fell first. The 7.62x51 NATO slug ripped through the goggles he wore to protect his eyes from dust. The left eyepiece shattered under the impact, the bullet plowing through his eye and out the back of his head. He dropped like a puppet with cut strings.

The second man pitched forward with a third eye, this one blood red, in the middle of his forehead.

The last man, the one in the lead, must have sensed something, because he looked back, skidding to a stop.

"He's yours if you want him, Reaper One," Cara said.

The cartel shooter only looked at his dead comrades in arms for a moment, then pivoted with the AK-12 rifle coming up.

Six-foot-four John Kane, with a grim reaper tattoo on his back earning him the name "Reaper", triggered a full-auto burst from his Heckler & Koch 416 carbine, sending a stream of 5.56mm slugs into the man's belly first then stitching a line across his chest. The cartel gunner dropped flat.

"All clear," Cara announced.

"For now," Kane said. "Regroup at the rally point."

"Copy."

Reaper, Axe and Arenas left the cacti and continued across the desert at a quick sprint.

So much for a sneak and peek recon, Kane thought.

Cara had insisted on covering Kane, Axe and Arenas just in case, and Kane hadn't argued because "just in case" had saved his backside many times over the years. You didn't survive as a Recon Marine, and then as the leader of Team Reaper, by taking unnecessary chances. He knew his enemy well.

In this case, the cartel had taken over a small village. "Taken over" might be too strong a term. Team Reaper's intelligence suggested the town willingly surrendered its farming areas to the cartel for the purposes of establishing poppy fields. The farms then supplied raw material to the cartels that they refined into opium and then heroin that made its way into the United States and around the globe.

In exchange, the residents received a cut of the profits. And the *narcos* let them live.

Team Reaper's mission was to wipe out the growing fields and cripple production in the southern region, as well as take down the man in charge, a cartel thug named Freddy Zalazar, aka *el-Jefe.*

Easier said than done.

Kane and his crew were not alone in the effort. Mexico's best federal anti-drug team, led by a Captain Rico Ramirez, who had helped Team Reaper before, were on the case as well. There were plenty of good guys to take on the endless supply of bad guys.

Kane's "rally point" was a makeshift camp in the shadow of a tall mountain, mostly centered in a nook that kept the back of the camp covered and all security focused on the front. If the cartel thugs wanted to climb the mountain behind them to try an attack from that direction, more power to them.

Kane, Axe and Arenas approached the two sentries at the perimeter. They were from Ramirez's squad. Kane gave the verbal code signal, and the sentries let them pass. Twenty yards ahead, a cluster of tents and portable equipment containers waited. Off to the left, a line of Desert Patrol Vehicles sat under a tarp. They were only the preliminary force. The rest of the unit would fly in via helicopter once their full-fledged attack began.

From one of the equipment containers, a bundle of wires stretched across the ground into one of the larger tents. A generator hummed beside the big tent. That was their command space.

Kane dismissed Axe and Arenas and found Rico Ramirez in the command tent. He leaned on a small table with both hands, studying a set of photographs on the tabletop.

"How we doing?" Kane said. He slung his weapon. Kane had to hunch a little otherwise he bumped his head on the low canvas ceiling. There were drawbacks to being tall. Kane had learned to live with them.

Ramirez had no such issue, standing only five-ten with a mop of dark hair on his head and a wiry frame. He was all muscle and bone and his tan fatigues fit tightly.

He stood as Kane reached him and gestured to the photographs.

"Latest sat recon from El Paso," Ramirez said.

Team Reaper's headquarters was located in El Paso, Texas, where Team Bravo and the rest of Kane's support crew handled intelligence and other matters, including the operation of armed Predator drones that often came in handy.

"These pics show the poppy fields, four of them, about fifty klicks south of the village."

"These other pictures the village itself?"

"Yeah. Lots of adobe and wood. The people who live there like living off the grid and away from the rest of society. There's not a lot of work, so they're prime targets for the cartels."

"Why do gunners stand around like they're operating a prison camp?"

"There's always one or two who object," Ramirez said. "They keep everybody under a gun to make sure those objections don't turn into action."

"Can we count on anybody in the village to help?"

"Probably the opposite," Ramirez said. "We're destroying their livelihood. They'll fight along with the cartel shooters. We might be looking at something far worse than we anticipated."

CHAPTER 8

"I'M NOT in the habit of shooting civilians," Kane said. "I shoot enough people as it is."

And there was that one time...

"We might not have a choice, Reaper," Ramirez said.

Kane only blinked a few times as Ramirez, the hardened drug fighter, looked at him. But Kane had no response. He was a warrior, and warriors fought. Warriors *felt*, too. They weren't machines. Kane had no qualms about killing evil men, but civilians who were fighting to protect their dignity and their property was something entirely different. It didn't matter to them if their property included drug farms. It was *theirs*. It wasn't somebody else's to destroy.

They were being used by the cartels who counted on such reactions.

They were pawns in a larger conflict. Cannon fodder. Because the cartels *didn't* care who died.

"What happens to these people," Kane said, "after we blow up their poppy farms?"

"There's a new government program to re-teach these farmers how to grow crops and be successful selling them," Ramirez said, "but the success rate has been low so far. It's easier to farm drugs."

"Ain't that a shame?"

Ramirez offered a sad shrug. "That's Mexico."

Kane checked his watch. "When do the choppers get here?"

"Another thirty minutes."

"Good. After today's skirmish, they're going to be waiting for us. We need to hit and git."

Footsteps behind him. Kane turned to see Cara Billings standing at the tent entrance.

"Room for one more?" she said.

"Just going over some logistics," Kane said. She joined them at the table. They had been lovers once, but that thread was now dead between them. They remained good friends.

———

The choppers were ten minutes out.

Ramirez and his crew, along with all five members of Team Reaper, pulled the tarps off a line of Desert Patrol Vehicles and hopped aboard. Ramirez rode with Kane; Cara with Axe; and Carlos with Richard "Brick" Peters, the team's medic. The rest of Ramirez's team paired up as well, and the line of DPVs took off from the camp site and headed for the target area.

They spread out as they traveled over the rough land, navigating various obstacles and small hills. Kane's sunglasses shielded his eyes from the dust and natural debris, but he felt the kicked-up desert sand scratching at the exposed portions of his neck and face.

In his lap rested the freshly-oiled and fully-loaded Heckler & Kock 416. Ramirez, behind the wheel, had stowed his weapon between the front seats.

The desert flashed by, rolling beneath the thick tires, the stiff suspension and carbon-fiber seats making for a rough ride, but it was over soon enough. The vehicles stopped in a row halfway up a hill, Kane, Ramirez, and the rest piling out to drop flat at the top of the hill.

Below, spread out over the length of a football gridiron, were the poppy fields. And the troops watching over them.

The plan called for Team Reaper and the Mexican Anti-Drug squad to wait for the choppers to begin their first pass and drop the remaining members of the home country strike force. Kane and Ramirez would then lead their squads around the hill to continue the engagement.

Kane checked his watch and turned his head skyward. Three dots on the horizon. The choppers were inbound.

Cara, to the right of Kane in fatigues and combat gear, her HK in both hands, said, "Do you get the feeling there are more troops on the ground here than we anticipated?"

"Thanks to our mishap today, not surprised."

"Trigger fingers will get a workout for sure," Axe said, who was off to Kane's left.

"Everybody steady," Kane said. He set his HK down and removed from his rucksack a M320 grenade launcher, popping open the breech to load a high-explosive projectile.

The quad set of poppy fields were laid out side-by-side, divided into squares by walkways cut into the fields. Nobody on harvest duty right now; the fields were yet to reach that stage. But they were well on their way.

Kane eyed a wooden building on the west end of the field. The command shack. They had a radio there. That building had to be taken out before the fight started.

He lifted the sights of the M320, calculating the distance on the fly, as the choppers flew closer and the first echoes of their whipping rotor blades reached the fields.

Cartel troopers raced out of the command shack, yelling, troopers already in the field raising their weapons to the incoming flying machines. Single-shots cracked from their rifles.

Kane triggered his grenade. With a thump the high-explosive round left the launch tube, its arc carrying it over the field. The projectile landed slightly off target, but the explosion achieved the desired effect.

Half the shack went up in flames, the blast also knocking down the radio tower behind the building. Two figures, their clothes aflame, stumbled out of the building, their screams almost overpowering the automatic weapons fire as they tumbled onto the dirt.

The choppers swooped overhead, door-mounted machine guns hammering at the ground troops. Kane gave a shout, and left the hillside with his team behind him.

It made no sense to run over the top of the hill and risk a fall, and associated injury, while running into the battle zone. A carve-out between the hill on which they rested and a neighboring rise provided a path of travel to the poppy fields, and they raced through the narrow space before the enemy had time to realize they were coming. Cartel guns were still aimed at the choppers.

Kane, leading the way, opened fire as he cleared the carve-out, breaking right as planned so Cara, Axe, Carlos and Brick could take care of their own business.

Kane radioed to Ramirez that they were through the gap, and Rico responded that he and his crew were now on the way as well.

Enemy shooters turned their attention from the choppers to the new arrivals. Kane gripped his HK tight and prepared to meet them head-on.

CHAPTER 9

THE BULBOUS POPPIES, most still white but others starting to show shades of pink as they began to bloom, reached waist-level in height, so at least they didn't have the difficulty of tall plants to deal with. The enemy was easy to spot. Several had already fallen to the hammering machine guns in the chopper, but as Kane opened fire on a trooper, he was aware of the choppers now hovering, and other operators, Rico's crew, dropping from zip lines to the ground.

Kane charged forward, perpendicular to the poppies, firing at troops at the far end while the rest of his team engaged their own targets. The two cartel gunners in Kane's sights brought their guns up. Kane dived and rolled into the poppies, hearing them crunch beneath him as bullets split the air above him. He returned fire. One dropped, the other took cover same as Kane, but kept his head up a little too high. Not high enough to make a good target, but high enough to see where he was. Kane began low-crawling to get a better shot.

At the burning command shack, Cara and Axe approached the building, staying low to avoid the black smoke and flames. They peered in through a window on the non-damaged side, but there was nobody else within, and the radio equipment was completely destroyed. All they needed to do was wait for the fire to consume the rest of the building.

Automatic weapons fire continued to crackle as Team Reaper and Ramirez's squads took on cartel troopers. As Cara and Axe took cover, her eyes shifted to the west—where the village was.

"What do you think about the town?" she said.

"I ain't shooting civilians," Axe said.

Cara fired on a cartel gunner about to strike Ramirez as he tangled hand-to-hand with another shooter, the struggle ending as her slugs found their mark. With a savage smack, Ramirez dropped his opponent and triggered a burst from his weapon into the man's chest.

The choppers continued firing their heavy weapons. The battle was almost over.

"Let's hope it doesn't come to that," Cara said, removing her rucksack. She unzipped the top and pulled out two thermite bombs. She handed one to Axe.

"Come on!" she shouted. She and Axe ran from the burning building and back into the fight. They were going to plant the thermite bombs at either end of the poppy fields and let the consuming fire that resulted take care of the rest.

John Kane continued moving his body over the poppies, his target getting closer. He was so focused on the man ahead that he missed another shooter coming up on his right. He rolled almost too late as a burst from the shooter's Kalashnikov kicked dirt into his face. On his side, he let the HK fire, the volley stitching a circular pattern of red holes into the shooter's chest. Kane twisted around to the original target, only to see the man rushing him. Kane blasted a hole in one of the shooter's knees. He tumbled to the ground, landing on his rifle, and Kane put another round through his head as the man's breath left him in a rush.

Movement on his left. He snapped the HK that way. Cara, carrying her thermite bomb, ran alongside the field, heading for the far end.

Looking around, Kane saw very few cartel gunners still on their feet, and a lot of damage. The burning command shack continued to send black smoke skyward; the poppy fields had been churned by the choppers' machine guns, and it seemed as if the extra force had mattered little.

Rico Ramirez waved to him. Kane waved back and said over the radio, "How we look?"

"Field secured. The pilots say there's activity in the town. People heading this way."

Kane jogged to the Captain. "How long till they get here?"

"Who knows if they will."

"Shooters?"

"Doesn't seem to be any. I think all the shooters were here."

The choppers pulled away to touch down on the flat area of ground on the west side of the field. Cara and Axe reported their thermite bomb placed and set for five minutes.

"Get to the choppers!" Kane ordered. Ramirez echoed the exclamation, and the two forces ran for the trio of helicopters waiting to take them out of the combat zone.

Kane looked back. No civilians rushing to them. He hoped they were gathered around the edge of town only to wonder what to do. They certainly weren't going to go running into a gun battle without weapons of their own. Kane ran ahead. He hoped the government program Ramirez had referenced would help the people of the village earn an honest living.

Otherwise, the cartel would be back. The farmers would be waiting. And willing to continue the enterprise.

In the end, that happened anyway. Kane had lost count of how many battles he'd fought against the drug thugs because the war never stopped. Today, they destroyed a poppy field. Tomorrow, another would be planted. Maybe someday, the farm they had just destroyed would be revitalized.

A never-ending cycle.

The thermite bombs detonated as the choppers rose, kicking up a miniature sandstorm, but the blast of machine-generated wind only fanned the flames.

The poppies disintegrated under the intense heat of the two fires that joined into one as Kane's chopper left the ground, his team safely aboard, nobody wounded, but looking plenty dirty after playing in the desert.

As the chopper rose, the altitude gave him a good look at the village, and the dirt road leading from it to the poppy field. There were people rushing along the road to the farm, but they only carried pitch forks and axes. Kane shook his head.

The air was still enough and the ground dry enough that the fire in the poppy field wouldn't spread to the town. The people weren't running to protect their village. They were running to protect poison.

Like Ramirez had said, that was Mexico.

CHAPTER 10

THE FARMS MIGHT RETURN, but there was one way to make sure it took a while, if ever, to actually happen.

The top cock in charge of the southern region was Freddy Zalazar, who went by *el-Jefe*, and his mansion sat atop a small hill a few miles away. He had the advantage of a paved road leading from the mansion to wherever he needed to go, and as the three choppers followed that road, the pilot in the lead reported a caravan of vehicles speeding in their direction.

Kane and Team Reaper were strapped into hard metal seats in the chopper's cabin, with Ramirez and some of his squad sitting opposite. Kane and Ramirez only exchanged glances before Rico said, "They're heading for the village. Use rockets on the road. If they hit the caravan, that's a bonus."

Kane smiled. Rico thought exactly like him. No quarter, no mercy.

The lead chopper dived as the pilot aimed for the

road, the gunner beside him zeroing his gunsight on the center median. Rockets flashed from the side-mounted pods, and a large section of the pavement exploded. The caravan, still around 100 meters away, came to a screeching halt, a perfect target for the door gunner, who gave the vehicles a burst from his .50-caliber Browning machinegun. The salvo hit the vehicle in front the hardest, nearly splitting the car down the middle. The remaining rounds punched neat round holes through the roofs of the other two cars.

"Nice work," Ramirez said into the radio.

Kane glanced at team. They sat to the right of him. Their eyes showed they were still eager for a fight. Eager to close down el-Jefe, his poppy fields, and anything and anyone else that stood in their way.

"Five minutes out," Ramirez said.

Kane used the time to switch channels on his com unit and radio headquarters in El Paso.

General Mary Thurston, the overall team leader of the Reaper effort, answered the call right away.

"Anybody hurt?"

"No, ma'am," Kane said. "We're on our way to el-Jefe now. Just took out some of his goons making for the village."

"Keep me posted. We're watching on satellite."

"Copy."

Ramirez held up two fingers. Kane yelled for his crew to get ready. He leaned out the open door, looking over the machine gunner's shoulder at the view ahead. The white mansion lay ahead. Already small dots that Kane knew were men with guns were rushing to the defense.

A puff of smoke near the edge of el-Jefe's property meant only one thing.

"Missile incoming!" Kane shouted.

The first missile flashed by the three helicopters, flying wide.

The second struck Kane's chopper.

The heat-seeker traveled between the two choppers in front. The pilots in the lead broke off left and right, letting flares go to fool the missile, but the countermeasures deployed by the third chopper on which Team Reaper and Rico Ramirez flew did not fool the projectile.

The rocket slammed into helicopter beneath the cabin, the blast rocking the chopper and hurling it toward the ground.

Kane and company held tight as the pilot tried to steer the helicopter as it dropped, leveling off slightly as the ground grew dangerously large below them. The gunner was dead, his side of the chopper having taken the direct hit.

Smoke filled the cabin as Kane and company, strapped into their seats, held onto whatever they could grab to keep from falling from the machine. The ground rushed closer.

The chopper hit hard, the first impact straining the seat restraints that held the cabin crew in place, and then the chopper slid along the desert ground until it finally came to a stop.

Kane hit the quick-release for his restraints and jumped out of his seat, hurrying to aid the rest of his team as they unbuckled and grabbed for stray equipment. Ramirez, winded, checked the pilot, only to note that he had gone through the windshield on impact. If it hadn't been for him controlling the crash, they might have all met the same fate, Ramirez pointed out. Team Reaper didn't argue.

"We're on foot!" Kane shouted as he and the rest of the crew continued their assault. They ran along the road. Fighting had already begun, with the remaining two choppers subduing resistance with .50-cal heavy-machinegun fire.

"There better be somebody left to kill!" Brick Peters shouted as they ran.

"Bet on it!" Kane yelled back.

Nobody tried to kill John Kane and lived to try again.

And they had two pilots to avenge.

Payback time.

———

Every pass the choppers made with the .50-cals hammering lessened the fight. As Team Reaper and Ramirez and his squad raced up the incline to the wrought-iron fence at the perimeter of the mansion, most of the house fighters were dead or dying, spread out on the paved area in front of the house that contained a water-fountain and several marble statues.

As Kane and his crew hopped over the fence, HKs probing for targets, the artistic layout wasn't what caught Kane's eye.

He noticed, right away, the garage on the left side of the house. Especially because a car crashed through the garage door before it had the time to fully open on its automatic track.

El-Jefe was in that car.

Kane, conscious of the rest of his team spreading out to assist the anti-drug squad, lifted his rifle to his shoulder and fired.

CHAPTER 11

THE BURST of 5.56mm slugs only bounced off the high-powered Lincoln; none of the slugs penetrated the bodywork, or smashed the back window.

"Reaper Two," Kane shouted as he broke into a run for the garage.

"Go!" Cara said over the radio.

"Our target is getting away. I'm taking off in pursuit. Coordinate with Captain Ramirez."

"Copy, Reaper One."

Kane swung the HK into the garage, scanning quickly left to right. No threats. There were other vehicles waiting, a selection of high-performance cars, two big Land Rovers, and three motorcycles. Kane slung his rifle and selected one of the motorcycles, a bright red sport bike. Without a key. Kane hurriedly searched and found the keys on a peg board near the door to the house. He grabbed the keys to the sport bike and fired the motor and took off after the Lincoln.

The rush of hot air as he pushed the sport bike to full throttle dried the sweat on his neck and face, Kane kept the Lincoln in sight. It was easy. The road was straight and well-paved and heading into the mountains. Kane didn't know what lay beyond, but he had no intention of letting el-Jefe get there. His fancy bulletproof Lincoln was going to meet its end, with him inside, well before.

And Kane had an idea how to make it happen.

Freddy Zalazar, aka el-Jefe, had always taken his position as top dog in the southern cartel seriously, with his operations not only including sending narcotics elsewhere than the United States, but human trafficking as well. He kept an eye on the tourist areas for the right kind of women to kidnap.

As he sat in the back of the speeding Lincoln, the only thing he could think of was that there were more than only Mexicans in the attacking helicopters, and the man on the bike wasn't brown, either.

The Americans were here.

The Lincoln's bulletproof glass would only protect him for so long.

Next to him, on the phone to the hidden airfield where Zalazar kept a jet, Esmerelda Jimenez shouted orders at the crew on the other end of the line. While Zalazar was short and stout, his clothes fitting loose over his thick body, she was tall and slender with black-painted nails and an automatic rifle always within reach. Her favorite weapon, a short-barreled Galil ACE in 7.62x39mm, was on the seat next to her. Her blue pantsuit fit her trim figure well, accentuating her wide hips.

As she spoke, Zalazar watched the man on the sport bike. He was getting closer. Zalazar knew how fast that bike could go, and knew the heavier Lincoln was no match. Bulletproof, yes but otherwise easy to catch with such a small and lightweight machine.

Zalazar tapped Esmerelda's shoulder. She shushed him and continued yelling into the phone.

"Esmerelda."

"Shush!"

"Esmerelda!"

The rider drew a pistol and extended it at the back of the Lincoln, firing a trio of rounds, all three bouncing off the back glass with solid thuds. Zalazar screamed anyway, and that finally got Esmerelda's attention, although her scowl wasn't the kind of glance he wanted from her. She ended the conversation and grabbed the Galil and told him to get on the floor if he was so frightened, while she dealt with the problem in her preferred manner.

She yelled for the driver to open the roof. The driver pressed the button, and a section of the roof pulled back to let in a blast of warm air. Esmerelda extended the Galil's collapsible stock, and then rose through the opening in the roof, planting her long legs on the seat while she rested her bottom on the forward edge of the roof. Her black hair flew around her face, but that didn't seem to bother her aim.

Zalazar watched Esmerelda sight along the barrel and pull the trigger. Flame flashed from the ACE and 7.62mm brass rained into the car, Zalazar raising a hand to keep the hot brass from falling onto him. The raised hand didn't keep one from falling down the back of his shirt, and he let out another yell, squirming to make the shell drop to the small of his back where he could reach it.

Tossing the shell aside, el-Jefe leaned forward to look out the window. The burst hadn't knocked down the rider, but it had forced him to back off a little.

Then he zoomed close again and his pistol cracked in response.

————

The woman's black hair whipped around her face as she rose from the opening in the roof, but that didn't stop her very accurate burst of fire from almost knocking John Kane off the sport bike.

He dodged left, then right, as she appeared, the salvo still coming very close and smacking into the blacktop where his wheels had been seconds before. One of the bullets tugged at the side of his right boot.

He knew the 9mm stingers from his SIG-Sauer M-17 autoloader wouldn't hurt the Lincoln any more than his blast from the HK 416 had, but it did achieve one desired result. He now had a big hole in the roof to take advantage of.

The enemy couldn't shoot through those bullet-proof windows. Breaking bulletproof glass, even if you could, to shoot through the resulting opening kind of defeated the whole purpose. And since el-Jefe needed protection, Kane knew the Mexican Amazon body-guard would do a pop goes the weasel impression.

Kane increased speed with the SIG pistol in hand and fired again, three fast shots, two striking the back window and the third going high enough to make the woman with the machine gun duck for cover.

Kane put away the SIG and grabbed a grenade from his web belt. He took his hands off the wheel long enough to pull the pin, then put his left hand on the handlebar, keeping the grenade in his right with the spoon firmly pressed against the orb.

The dark-haired woman rose from the roof opening again, Kane swinging the motorbike to the right as she opened fire, her salvo tearing another scar on the black-top. He accelerated toward the back passenger fender as the woman shifted her aim. He tossed the grenade. Her eyes widened at the sight of the explosive as it travelled to car, but the toss fell short. The grenade bounced off the side of the roof, onto the road. Kane swerved left but felt the shockwave of the blast pushing at his back. He grabbed for the SIG.

The woman swung the Galil at him again, Kane triggering a double-tap that slammed into her chest. She screamed and let go of the Galil, Kane firing another shot that smashed through the center of her face. She fell to the side, half-in and half-out of the car, until el-Jefe pushed her out entirely. Kane swerved right to avoid her tumbling body.

The Lincoln tried to speed up, and actually pulled away from Kane a bit, but once he holstered his M-17 and applied pressure to the throttle, the sport bike regained the lead.

Kane took out another grenade and pulled the pin. The Lincoln started to swerve left and right, the driver trying to use the back end to knock Kane off the road, but Reaper One held tight and tossed the grenade.

Slam dunk, hole in one, whatever you wanted to call it. The grenade passed through the gap in the roof and that's when Kane finally hit the brakes, the tires smoking, the rubber leaving a black streak on the blacktop as the Lincoln continued on.

Kane held fast in case el-Jefe managed to pick up the grenade and throw it out.

But that didn't happen.

Instead, the rear of the car exploded.

The orange flame blasted out the bulletproof glass and sent a plume of flame through the moon roof. The front end of the car careened out of control, bouncing off the road and slammed to a stop in a ditch.

The secondary blast torched the front end.

Kane didn't spend any time inspecting the kill.

He turned the sport bike the other way and took off. He had to rejoin his team and Rico Ramirez. They still had work to do at the late el-Jefe's mansion.

———

"Why does Reaper get to do all the cool stuff?" Axe wanted to know.

Cara Billings, Reaper Two, raised an eyebrow to Axel Burton. The ex-Recon Marine was a qualified sniper, same as her, solidly built, in his early thirties.

Axe and Cara had a friendly "sniper rivalry". She liked to say she could shoot the fly off a horse's back; Axe joked he could shoot the fly before it landed on the horse. It was the kind of competition that kept them both sharp and in practice.

But in combat, all jokes went by the wayside. When it counted, they backed up each other and saved the jokes for when the danger passed. And hopefully they all survived.

Cara wondered if Axe was really upset that Kane

had taken off on the bike or if he was upset about having to pull guard duty at the mansion when there were ladies to chase. He'd already noticed several attractive women within Ramirez's unit that he wanted to get to know better.

"I don't know what he's thinking," Cara admitted, summing up her entire relationship with Kane. The rocky on again off again relationship they'd maintained for far too long was finally off for good, but they still shared a common bond, that of protecting people close to them, and not, in this case, their teammates. Cara had a son, in hiding, that she spoke to every night. Kane had his sister, still in a coma, to think about too. She was hidden away as well, under an assumed name.

Their enemies had far too long a reach for them not to maintain such security precautions.

Then they heard the boom.

Axe nodded in the direction of the road Kane had traveled. "Sounds like he blew up that Lincoln."

Cara turned to look. The column of black smoke against the tan desert and blue sky could not be denied.

As long as it wasn't Kane and the sport bike on fire.

But she didn't say that out loud.

She and Axe stood on the eastern edge of the mansion property. The choppers had landed on the flat ground nearby. There wasn't room in the front patio area for choppers to land. Rico Ramirez and his crew began taking empty boxes from the two remaining choppers, which they took inside and were, now and then, carrying out, full, and stacking. Cara figured they were raiding the place for usable intelligence, but she had no idea what they were looking for.

Carlos and Brick covered the west side of the

mansion. There was no reason to think there would be a counter attack, but the crew was ready just in case.

The dead had been stacked at the rear of the house. Luckily only a few of the Ramirez crew had sustained wounds or injuries, and none of Team Reaper had been hurt, a testimony to their skill and experience at fighting cartels for far too long.

El-Jefe's troops hadn't stood a chance against the combined firepower of the Mexican Anti-Drug Squad, Team Reaper, and, especially, the .50 calibers from the choppers. They had lost the two pilots of the downed helicopter, though. The day wasn't without loss.

The fancy courtyard/patio combination had not fared well either. Most of the fountain lay in pieces, water having splashed all around the feature.

The marble statues were either headless, armless, or had kept their arms and heads but had a series of holes throughout the rest of their figures.

Cara noted the missile battery at the edge of the courtyard still contained two of four missiles. The firing console, connected to the battery by a series of cables and situated away from the back blast of the rockets, remained undamaged.

Cara heard an annoying buzzing sound.

"Sounds like Reaper," she said.

They shifted closer to the rail of the courtyard that offered a view of the long roadway and the house garage. John Kane, still atop the sport bike, looking no worse for wear, zoomed toward the mansion.

Kane slowed as he started up the incline to the garage, finally stopping the bike and cutting the motor. Cara and Axe went to him as he swung his legs off the vehicle.

"How'd it go?" Axe said.

"Stick a fork in el-Jefe," Kane said. "He's no longer pink in the middle."

Cara noted two missing grenades on Kane's webbing and figured out how he had disposed of the cartel leader, but there were other questions on her mind other than Zalazar's final moments.

"What the hell are we doing standing around here, Reaper?"

"Rico didn't say?"

"Neither did you, in the briefing," Axe pointed out.

"Well, Zalazar didn't only run drugs. He was into kidnapping and human trafficking. Part of Rico's mission is to get any intel related to kidnappings, people smuggling routes, that sort of thing."

"And we're playing security guard while they do that?"

"We didn't exactly get an invitation to come here, guys," Kane said. "We had to wheel and deal a little. Part of the deal was we stand down while they loot the place."

Cara stifled her reply. She was glad some effort was being made against human smugglers, but she sure would have liked a crack at them herself.

The voice of Carlos, loud and full of alarm, came over their com units.

"We got incoming! Two choppers incoming!"

CHAPTER 12

"THEY DON'T LOOK FRIENDLY," was all Brick said as he and Arenas watched the helicopters close the distance. They weren't close enough to engage.

Rico Ramirez came running over, stopping close to the Reaper pair. With a pair of binoculars, he examined the approaching helicopters.

"They aren't ours," he said.

Ramirez began shouting orders to his men to prepare for an attack. Brick offered to man the missile battery. Rico told him OK and Kane didn't argue. Brick, the team medic, the exposed portions of his arms covered with tattoos, ran across the patio to where the missile battery sat.

Slinging his HK, he examined the control console. A joystick rotated the battery. A crude sighting system built into the unit's radar signaled when a target was locked. With the joystick he swung the missiles in the direction of the approaching choppers.

"Don't fire, Brick," Kane ordered over the radio.

"They aren't friends, Reaper."

"Wait till Ramirez gives the order."

"And if they shoot first?"

"Then let 'em rip."

Brick let out a short laugh. Easiest order in the world.

He flicked a switch that primed both rockets.

Cara and Axe volunteered to go to the roof with their sniper rifles. Three stories up wasn't much of a high ground, but they might have a chance at knocking down the helicopters with their high-powered HK rifles. Kane gave them the go-ahead.

The incoming choppers continued toward the mansion, heading for the west side. Kane and Arenas crouched at the west side deck railing, the wall of the mansion behind them, the French doors leading to the deck already open to provide means of retreat and more cover.

Members of Ramirez's squad also lined the rail. They'd open on the choppers as soon as the flying machines were in range, but they knew that if the choppers were close enough for small arms, they were all close enough for the mounted weapons the helicopters carried. Ramirez identified at least one rotary machine gun on the lead helicopter; the other looked only equipped for transport.

Kane's finger tightened on the trigger as the hot sun beat down.

Any second...

"What do you say, Reaper One?" Brick said over the radio.

Kane glanced at Rico, who nodded curtly.

"Knock 'em down, Brick."

———

Valdo Mendez chuckled at the line of troops massing to try and shoot down his helicopters.

Hired by Chucho Banderas and Victor Zamorano to take out the annoying pest known as Team Reaper, Mendez zeroed the rotary machine gun on the right side of the helicopter, the side on which he sat, while the pilot kept the chopper on course with the mansion.

Behind him, his specialist crew of mercenaries stood ready to fast-rope to the ground and take on the Mexican federal agents and Americans up close.

Mendez's helicopter was only responsible for air support. His job was to watch the slaughter and report back.

But nobody had told him *el-Jefe* had put missiles on his patio.

Mendez didn't have to tell the pilot anything as the first rocket left the battery and streamed toward the helicopter. His kingdom for an automatic targeting computer on the machine gun, however. He might have been able to knock down the rocket.

Instead, the pilot took evasive action, cutting right, then sweeping left, trying to cut across the top of the rocket as it neared. The seat straps strained against Mendez's body as the tight turns tossed him back and forth, but the missile went by. The pilot turned so Mendez could see the other chopper, which had dropped in altitude, and was now racing the final distance to the mansion.

"Get us back on course," Mendez said. The enemy on the ground was already firing, and then movement on the roof of the mansion caught his attention. "Snipers!" he said. "Hold steady."

The pilot complied while Mendez used his right hand to work the firing mechanism of the rotary machine gun. His index finger pressed the trigger.

———

Cara and Axe climbed a ladder through the attic to the roof, shoving open a trap door that allowed access to the top of the mansion. The flat roof was a plus, as was the cover provided by air conditioning units. The metal boxes might not be good for stopping bullets, but they provided a nice rest for high-powered rifles.

They set up across from each other, locking the folding bipods in place, Cara flicking the covers off her scope. The magazine was fully charged with 7.62mm NATO steel-tipped rounds, and she watched the helicopters avoid the first missile as she put her finger on the trigger. The choppers did not appear to have any armor. The steel-tipped rounds would easily cut through their metal skins.

The HK M110A1 was a fine rifle, and very comfortable to hold, with a grip angle very similar to the 416 carbine they used regularly.

"Who are these guys?" Axe said.

"Less talking, more shooting."

"Somebody needs to teach Brick how to fire a missile."

"Shut up and *shoot*, Axe!"

Automatic weapons fire erupted from the lower

deck level as the gathered troops opened up, the choppers finally in range. Cara sighted on the helicopter with the mountain machinegun. As the pilot steadied the nose on the roof, she understood she and Axe had been spotted. She fired, squeezing off three rounds in rapid succession, Axe contributing his own rounds. Two struck the canopy glass, long spider cracks announcing solid hits. Through her scope, Cara watched the spark of another round flashing off one of the landing skids.

The chopper pitched away, the rotary machine gun spitting flame. The ripping noise of the multi-barrel rotary cannon almost drowned out every other weapon. Cara braced as the house shook, the line of rounds impacting with the upper levels of the mansion, tearing into the walls.

That meant debris. A lot of it. Falling on the lower deck where Kane, Arenas, Ramirez and the rest of the Mexican anti-drug operators were still shooting.

Cara swung her HK rifle right, tracking the armed chopper. She fired twice. Axe followed up with another pair of shots.

"Aim for the engine!" Axe shouted.

Cara adjusted her aim, firing, a clear miss. She tried to follow the chopper as it turned left, but it flew too fast for her to pivot along. She looked up, watching the chopper turn away in a long circle. *Now.* She placed the crosshairs of her scope ahead of the nose, fired twice. Two neat holes appeared in the body. But had the rounds been effective?

We're throwing rocks at a tank. Armor or not, those choppers weren't coming down the easy way.

———

Kane and Carlos didn't let up on their HKs' triggers as the rotary cannon let off its buzz saw-like sound and stitched the wall behind them full of holes. The cannon slugs knocked out chunks of the wall, which came sailing to the lower floor deck. Bits of sheetrock pelted Kane's back.

Arenas screamed and fell from the deck rail. Kane knelt beside him. "I'm fine!"

A piece of the wall had smacked him in the back. Kane tossed the chunk aside and helped Arenas back to his feet.

The second missile from the patio battery, the last, flew overhead, Brick using the last option they had for knocking down one of the choppers.

The second chopper with the full cargo bay exploded with a direct hit. Everybody on the deck cheered as the chopper fell in two pieces and hit the desert ground hard, exploding a second time. A heat wave flashed over Kane and the others, and their attention turned to the remaining chopper.

The pilot showed no intention of bugging out.

"Nice shot, Reaper Five," Kane said into his com unit.

"It had better be after I screwed up the first. We still have one bogey outstanding, though."

"Reaper Two?" Kane said. "Do you or Four have a shot?"

"Too far," came Cara's reply. "We need him closer."

Kane turned to Ramirez as the Mexican drug cop helped some of his team to their feet.

"Anybody hurt?"

"Only a few scratches."

Cara: "Reaper One."

"Go, Two."

"He's coming back."

Kane reloaded his HK as the remaining helicopter turned back in the direction of the mansion.

"We need to get everybody inside," Kane said.

Ramirez agreed and started giving the order.

Part of his team ran around to the front of the mansion, while Kane, Arenas, Ramirez, and several other Mexican drug agents hustled for the French doors behind them.

Then the gunfire started again, the rotary flashing flame, the bright lines of tracer ammo smashing once again into the wall of the mansion.

"Find some cover!" Kane shouted.

He wondered if anything in the bedroom would be enough to protect from the incoming fusillade of death.

CHAPTER 13

THE TRACER ROUNDS hammered into the house, tearing through the walls with thunderous ferocity, slicing over the heads of the operatives hugging the floor in the bedroom. Hands covered necks, faces stayed in the carpet, and some yelled as debris landed on them. Anything in the path of the bullets was destroyed, the non-stop salvo shredding little trinkets and decorations and furnishings around the bedroom. Presently the swarm of hot lead finally ceased.

Rico Ramirez shouted, "Anybody dead?"

When Kane looked up, there were more holes in the roof than in the proverbial slice of Swiss cheese, but he also saw another sight that made him run to the now-ruined French doors and look out.

The transport choppers that had brought them to the mansion were finally airborne and pursuing the attacking helicopter, door gunners firing steadily, the lighter and more maneuverable attack helicopter quickly outpacing the larger transporters. Kane watched the helicopter shrink as it traveled away.

"You okay, Reaper?"

Kane turned. Arenas brushed off his uniform, the rest of the people in the room doing the same, Cara checking cuts on Axe's face, Brick, being the team medic, checking some of the wounded from Ramirez's team.

"Fine," Kane said.

"That was close."

"I have a bad feeling."

"What do you mean?"

"I don't think those guys"—he gestured to the still-burning chopper that had crashed, the one that Brick had shot down, as black smoke continued to drift from the wrecked fuselage—"were here to help Zalazar."

Arenas frowned. "You think we were set up?"

"I think somebody tried to take us out, yeah."

"Who?"

"Good question."

Kane removed his rucksack and moved out to the patio, where he kicked aside chunks of debris as he made his way to the damaged rail. He pressed a button on the com unit on his belt and said, "Reaper One to Bravo."

General Mary Thurston, back at their El Paso headquarters, did not answer.

"Reaper One to Bravo."

Silence.

"General, can you hear me?"

Cara called from behind him. "What's going on, Reaper?"

He turned to her.

"I can't reach HQ."

"Let me try."

Cara used her own com unit to try and raise General Thurston, but had no luck. The com units did not appear damaged. Kane and Cara quickly went to the other Team Reaper members, and nobody managed to reach home base.

Cara turned to Kane. "The link is dead."

Kane looked away from her, outside, in the direction the fleeing attack chopper had gone. "But why?" he said.

One thought came to mind. *Something bad is happening at home and there's not a damn thing we can do about it.*

World Wide Drug Initiative HQ, El Paso, TX

The black Boeing Vertol CH-46 Sea Knight flew over El Paso, staying low, the twin rotor blades of the speeding aircraft moving at a fast clip. A big man stood behind the pilot and co-pilot watching as their target, a warehouse near the El Paso Zoo, close to the 110 Highway, appeared through the Plexiglass screen.

"Set us down in the parking lot," the man said. His tone of voice, and his hulking appearance, made him a hard man to argue with. The pilot adjusted their course slightly, and the big man returned to the cabin where he shouted to his six-man assault team that they were minutes from landing.

"And a reminder. No prisoners. The building goes *down*."

Boris Yakovlev frowned as his men, mercenaries all, acknowledged his words with a collective shout. He did not like mercenaries. He didn't like being a mercenary. But that's what he was; that was the role life had selected for him. Lately, his specialist skills had been hired out by various drug cartels in Mexico.

He intended to play out his role in life until something better came along or he died. In the meantime, when his clients gave him specific instructions, he made sure to carry them out to such an exacting standard that he'd come up with a few details the client missed.

Such as in this case, blowing up a warehouse in El Paso, that served as the headquarters of a strike team the client wanted to get rid of. Permanently. Two cartel leaders named Zamorano and Banderas had personally hired him for this job, a project they considered of utmost importance.

Fine with Boris. They paid cash, in full, up front.

Yakovlev returned to the cockpit. The warehouse looked bigger now. It didn't seem that the people inside, the client's enemies, realized the helicopters were about to land and blast them to smithereens.

The big Russian knew from ground scouts that the warehouse had no guards, or anything that marked the building as that of a covert government strike force. The parking lot was too big for the small number of cars. Cameras on the roof scanned the parking area, and the surrounding streets, but did not cover a wide area, concerned mostly with only the outer perimeter.

The big Russian returned to the cabin to grab his battle pack and weapons from the corner he'd secured them before the flight.

He didn't want to exit the chopper without a machine gun in his hand.

By now, the ground team should have done their

part of the job, which would make Yakovlev's much easier.

———

General Mary Thurston stood in the operations center, the section of Team Reaper headquarters where Team Bravo manned computer workstations with satellite access, and put images on the wall-sized monitors at the front of the room.

Brooke Reynolds and Pete Teller sat behind two such workstations, noting information coming in from the Mexico operations and providing updates.

They watched Kane's and Ramirez's group deal fight off the attacking helicopters, General Thurston with her arms folded, wondering how Zalazar had managed to call the reinforcements after not only escaping so quickly, but also being dispatched as equally fast by John Kane.

The radio unit she wore on her belt tied her to Team Reaper via satellite, but she knew better than to chime in and see how they were doing.

At a workstation to her left sat Sam "Slick" Swift, the man with the golden fingers. He could not only hack anything with a microchip, he knew the computers at Reaper headquarters better than the people who had designed the systems. The thin redhead had a look of alarm on his face as he turned to Thurston.

"My screen shows two choppers closing fast, General."

Thurston turned from the wall monitors and looked over Swift's shoulder. Part of his workstation included the security camera feed, and one of the cameras on the roof showed the CH-46 twin-rotor choppers flying low over the neighboring El Paso Zoo.

"Civilian?" she said.

"Military surplus."

"How can you tell?" Thurston said.

"You can see on the paint where the Marine identification numbers have been removed."

Thurston blinked, examining the choppers on the screen. She couldn't tell. Chalk it up to Swift's above-average intelligence in such matters.

"We need to—" Thurston began, but she never finished the thought. The monitors on the walls ahead showing the satellite images from Mexico blinked out, fading to black.

She straightened. "What's going on?"

Then the lights went out. The room went totally dark. Only the low glow of exit signs provided illumination.

"Why isn't the generator working?" shouted Luis Ferrari as he exited his office and entered the operations room. At least, Thurston assumed he had entered. She couldn't see him.

Then the generator kicked on, but the work stations and monitors remained without power, and the lights that had been activated were meant to help them get out of the building, not maintain operations.

The sound of whipping rotor blades grew louder. There was no doubt the choppers were dropping into the parking lot.

"We're under attack!" Thurston shouted. "Guns, lights, find some cover! Somebody call the police!"

Thurston had six people at HQ; not all of them

knew how to fight. She hoped enough of them stayed in practice.

———

In the east section of the warehouse, separated by the operations center by a wall and the medical bay, Pete Traynor, known as Bravo Two, was cleaning his SIG pistol. He liked to hang around HQ when not in the field and spent a lot of time on the shooting range, keeping in practice for when Kane needed him in the field.

His face bore what some called a permanent five o'clock shadow. He whistled as he cleaned his pistol. His session had not been terrible, but he noted he needed to work on not jerking the trigger when he started to tire.

When the lights went out, he froze. He heard the choppers. The aircraft outside meant only one thing. Either Team Reaper was coming home early from Mexico, or somebody unpleasant was landing in the parking lot.

The light in the shooting range was dim, but he hurriedly reassembled the SIG and grabbed the spare magazines he had already cleaned and re-loaded after his practice session.

The swing-doors of the shooting range burst open with most of Team Bravo with General Thurston in the lead running in. Traynor helped them quickly gather HK 416s from racks on the wall, but there weren't enough pre-loaded magazines. Somebody spilled out a case of 5.56mm rounds while another grabbed a box of empty magazines, and the crew worked quickly on hands and knees to get rounds jammed into the 30-round box magazines before the pizza hit the fan.

"Are we being attacked?" Traynor said out loud.

"I think so," General Thurston said.

An explosion shook the floor. Everybody hit the deck. The walls shook and a few loose items dropped from shelves.

"I'd say you're right, ma'am," Traynor said.

"We gotta go!" Brooke Reynolds shouted, working the cocking handle on her HK. The group started for the doors, with a large pile of empty magazines and loose rounds still on the floor.

Traynor hoped what they had would be enough.

Because they didn't have much.

———

The CH-46 touched down but the rotors didn't stop. Boris Yakovlev threw open the port side sliding door, shouting for his men to follow him. His boots hit the tarmac and he ran for the warehouse, his team pounding the pavement behind him, each man prepared to meet heavy resistance. But if the reports from the cartel ground crew were for real, they wouldn't meet much. They faced only office personnel. It would be a slaughter.

Which is what the client wanted.

And Boris Yakovlev wasn't going to disappoint the cartel.

The big Russian carried an American M-16A2 with a tried-and-true M203 grenade launcher mounted under the barrel. While he knew the Russian Kalashnikov rifle was more reliable, he appreciated the American weapon's better accuracy. The rifle had been a constant companion for many campaigns, and the high explosive shell he fired from the M203 once again reaffirmed his love for the destructive device.

Intel said the door of the loading dock, on the right side of the building, was sealed off. A pair of double doors on the left side of the building front, were the ones used for entry and exit. Yakovlev aimed his grenade for those doors, and the resulting blast split the doors not only in half, but forced them off their hinges and into the interior as well.

Still running, getting closer, the big Russian fed another round into the M203 and fired from the hip. He knew how to hold the weapon to score the accuracy he needed, and this time did not disappoint. The HE shell sailed through the newly created opening and exploded inside, the bright flash of flame briefly lighting the interior and sending a plume of smoke into the afternoon air.

Yakovlev and his mercenaries flowed through the opening, weapons chattering, seeking the targets that scrambled throughout the building's limited space.

CHAPTER 14

DIM LIGHT. Thick smoke. Flames. Not quite sensory overload, Traynor decided as he jumped ahead of Brooke and Teller, the HK tucked into his shoulder and his eyes aligning the sights even though he couldn't see them. He was running on autopilot, counting on thousands of hours of practice to aim true.

As the assault force entered the building, the bright light of the doorway, mixing with the smoke, briefly highlighted them, and Traynor took advantage of the moment. The HK flashed flame as he worked the trigger, firing single shots only, shifting his aim with each shot. More gunfire behind him, some shouting, Team Bravo settling in for a fight. Traynor was well aware he saw more field action than any of them. They had a handicap he needed to help overcome.

The brightness behind the assault force turned to dark silhouettes as they moved deeper into the smoky warehouse, moving shadows now, their black combat outfits blending with the dim lighting. Their faces were blank, their shouting almost gibberish as tunnel vision took over Traynor's senses. The lack of light and the haze of smoke made the peripheral fading around his eyes worse.

Traynor saw two of the attackers fall from his initial salvo. He dived for the floor. At least, he hoped the floor was still there. He felt the hard floor beneath his feet, but saw only black. He landed as anticipated, sliding a few feet before coming to a stop. The glow from the open entrance helped him see shuffling legs. He fired in that direction. Somebody screamed.

More shooting behind him, Thurston's identifiable voice directing fire. Traynor coughed as he rose, smoke stinging his eyes, and he ran back in the direction of the General's commands. To run forward from his current spot meant he might be hit by friendly fire. Friendly fire *wasn't*.

Traynor dropped beside Luis Ferrero as a pistol discharged in Zero's right hand.

"They're heading into the operations center," Ferrero said.

"How can you tell?"

"Jesus, Traynor, where else is there to go?"

Return fire from the assault force peppered the walls around them, smacking hard, whining off metal pipes and snapping upward.

"They're here to blow the place," Traynor said. He fired at a muzzle flash. The muzzle flash only moved to the side. Ferrero fired at the same target. Somebody yelled.

"Nice shot, Zero."

"You think you're the only one who practices?"

The shooting died down for a moment, hushed

whispers from the enemy breaking through the fog. They were repositioning.

"We have to get in there and stop them," Traynor said.

Movement behind them, General Thurston low-crawling to them.

––––

In the operations section of the building, Boris Yakovlev issued hurried orders to the three of his crew who carried the C-4. The three men raced around the room, planting the explosive charges at every corner, while Boris ordered two more to charge around the corner and take out as many of the defenders as possible.

He checked his watch. Time was short, but they were ahead of schedule. The C-4 charges would destroy the section of the building where they stored critical data. Yakovlev wasn't interested in the shooting bay, medical area, or the miscellaneous portions of the warehouse where this U.S. government strike force conducted everyday business. The client wanted the heart ripped from the body, and the operations center was indeed that heart.

The two mercs he sent around the corner started shooting. Boris yelled for the rest to begin retreat as the three with the C-4 announced all charges had been placed and awaited remote detonation.

Yakovlev wasn't leaving the bombs to the potential unreliability of a timer.

––––

"We have an ammo problem," General Thurston said.

"No shit?" Traynor said.

If she gave him a disapproving look, Traynor couldn't see it in the dark haze they gathered within. "Brooke and Teller are out," she said, "Slick has one mag left, I'm down to one mag. What do you have?"

"Two mags," Traynor said, "and three for my pistol."

Thurston ordered everybody back behind the dividing wall between the shooting bay and the operations center, Traynor keeping his weapon downrange toward the enemy. She grabbed ammo from Swift, and her own, and gave the mags to Traynor and Ferrero. The two men were to cover the exit of the rest. There was a way out via an emergency exit beyond the shooting bay. Traynor and Ferrero would cover long enough for them to get away, then retreat as well.

"No arguing," Thurston said.

And then bullets ripped into her, tearing through her clothes and the skin beneath.

Two enemy troopers announced their charge around the corner with automatic fire and loud screams. They rushed headlong at the clustered Team Bravo. Thurston let out only a choked scream as she fell back, her blood spattering onto Traynor's face. Ferrero let out a yell as he fell against Traynor, who quickly scrambled out from under Zero's body and lifted the HK 416 over Ferrero's back. He shouted for Brooke, Teller and Swift to get out as he flicked the selector switch to full auto and fired out the magazine, the momentary burst of 5.56mm projectiles creating a strobe effect in the walkway.

One of the attackers dropped, but the other jumped

over his partner's body to continue the assault. Traynor grabbed the SIG M-17 from his hip holster. He aimed ahead of the moving shadow, his first two rounds bouncing off the wall beside the man, one finally finding its mark in the attacker's belly.

But the attacker only stopped short a moment, and his right hand moved in an underhand pitch. Traynor did not see what he tossed, but knew what was arcing their way. The SIG crashed again and the attacker's head snapped back. Before the man's body hit the floor, Traynor shouted, "Grenade!"

The blast shook the world around him and then Traynor fell into a black void.

CHAPTER 15

THE PHALANX of El Paso police officers, lights flashing, sirens creating a cacophony of noise throughout the neighborhood, sped toward the warehouse. Thick black smoke marked the location, the sudden blast of an explosion having filled the sky with fire. As the cops screeched into the parking lot, the left side of the building burned, the fire slowly moving to consume the untouched portion.

A helicopter had already left the scene, witnesses reporting the aircraft departing before the explosion, and as the cops jumped from their vehicles, they had no idea what to make of the situation. There were three ambulances down the block, standing by, but they weren't being allowed on the premises until the responding officers determined whether there was still an active threat at the location.

And then a man covered in blood stumbled from the exit.

———

Luis Ferrero felt heat.

The building was on fire. The smoke around him was thicker than before, and the increase in temperature meant only that the bombs he and Traynor had predicted, had gone off and fire consumed the operations center. They didn't have much time to escape. He wasn't even sure the others were still alive. The still body of Pete Traynor lay beside him, Mary Thurston moaned audibly behind him, and he couldn't see anybody else.

He tried to rise but collapsed. He'd been shot. His left leg throbbed; blood seeped from the lower left side of his belly.

He had to move. His teammates were counting on him.

He put his weight on his right leg and finally rose, crying out, coughing, as he bent at the waist, the wound in his belly hotter than the heat from the fires. Sweat dripped down his face. He wiped his eyes, keeping them closed against the sting of smoke.

He started forward. Slowly. The bright light of the destroyed exit guided him. He limped heavily on his left foot, falling flat on his face halfway. Crawling to the wall on his left, he used the wall to support his body and continued his trek. Closer. Closer to the exit. He felt the light touch of fresh air. He ignored the fire. He had to ignore the fire or succumb to it. His eyes were wide open. Pain flared through his body.

He reached the doorway and stumbled into the doorframe. His eyes cleared enough to see the line of police vehicles. He lifted a hand and screamed like a wounded animal. He took two steps from the doorway and collapsed again, pushing up on one arm as officers approached.

"We need help!" he shouted. "People inside!"

His vision began to fade. Ferrero heard a man shouting orders, and others responding to those orders, and relief flooded through him. Help was here. They weren't finished yet. And then Ferrero collapsed on the pavement with a loud smack and neither heard nor felt anything more.

―――――

Mexico

The two remaining transport choppers were crowded. Kane and his team, minus Brick who rode on the second chopper, shared the tight cabin space with members of Rico's squad and Captain Ramirez himself. In the second chopper, the overflow of Rico's team, plus the wounded, with Brick on hand to help with medical needs.

The engine was too loud for Kane to keep trying HQ on his portable com unit or pull out the emergency sat phone from his pack for a sure-fire connection. He stared into the far distance and wondered if the communication problem was more than a simple interruption.

A feeling deep down convinced him something awful had happened in El Paso, and he wouldn't settle down until he had an answer. A glance at Cara, Arenas, and Axe, with their own faraway looks, told him they felt the same way. Losing touch with home base for so long a period wasn't good at all.

The choppers eventually touched down at a police

airfield in Mexico City where the teams off-loaded, Kane and his crew gathering in a building near the main hangar that was their quarters for the duration of the mission. The shadow of the control tower loomed over the property. One side contained a table and sitting area, the other a set of bunk beds.

As they unloaded their gear, Kane removed the sat phone from his pack. Cara went into the restroom to change clothes while Axe and Arenas got out of their uniforms and into jeans and T-shirts while Kane dialed El Paso.

He stood in the corner of the sitting area near a window, listening for a connection that never happened.

He pulled the phone from his ear.

"Still nothing?" Axe said.

"Nothing at all," Kane admitted.

"We have to try Washington then," said Carlos.

Kane raised an eyebrow at the former Mexican Special Forces officer. Like him and Cara, Arenas had a family to think about; unlike Kane and Cara, his family included a spouse and not only children or a sibling trapped in a coma.

"You're right, Carlos."

Kane hated to say so, not because of any personal disagreement with Arenas, but because the square-jawed operator was reminding Reaper One of the emergency protocol, the protocol activated when home base was cut off, designed for a time should home base actually become *cut off*. Which meant home base might not exist any longer.

Kane dialed another number on the sat phone that would connect him to the Chairman of the Joint Chiefs of Staff in Washington, D.C. General Hank Jones. The General, in his late 60s, usually dealt only with Mary Thurston, who passed his instructions to Team Reaper. Kane liked Jones because, while the man might now ride a desk, he was a combat vet with the elite 75th Rangers. He knew what Kane and his crew dealt with in the field, and never failed to fully support their efforts.

The line connected.

"Yes?" Jones had a gruff voice. All business. Kane was calling on his private line per the protocol.

"Reaper One, sir."

"Why are you calling me, Reaper?"

"Emergency protocol, sir. Communications with El Paso have been cut off. We can't raise them on our com units or the sat phone."

"They don't answer?"

"The line is dead, sir. Are you aware of any incidents?"

"I am not," the General said. "Where are you?"

"Mexico."

"Mission in progress?"

"Mission accomplished and we're getting ready to go home."

"Stand by. I will investigate and get back with you. Don't go anywhere, Reaper."

The line clicked.

Kane set the sat phone on the table and looked blankly at Axe and Arenas, who stared back, and then Cara came out of the bathroom.

She saw the look on Kane's face and froze.

"You called Jones?" she said.

She knew the drill as well as the rest of them.

"Yeah," Kane told her. "He'll get back with us. We stand by in the meantime. One of you answer that phone if it rings." Kane started for the door. "I'll coordinate with Rico and let him know what's going on."

He went out, leaving the rest of his team in very uncomfortable silence.

CHAPTER 16

The Pentagon

GENERAL HANK JONES was a big man in his late 60s, and he wore an expression of concern as he tried to reach General Thurston in El Paso, also without success.

He looked out the window of his Pentagon office, then turned back to his computer. He searched through the military net for any distress notes from El Paso, but found none. He clicked on his web browser and typed EL Paso TX into the search bar.

He didn't know what he expected to find, but he straightened in his chair when he found it.

Articles about a warehouse explosion in El Paso. Police and fire crews responding. Unknown casualties. Reports of a helicopter leaving the scene prior to the blast.

The pictures from the *El Paso Times* left no question. The Team Reaper/Bravo warehouse had been torched. They needed to get assets in the area to secure the building and keep the local cops from sniffing too far.

Jones also needed to update the president.

He started making calls, reaching out to his staff to get on a plane and get to Texas and take control of the situation.

But he didn't need to call the president.

The president called him.

———

The White House, Oval Office

President Jack Carter, his grey hair slightly disheveled, looking all his sixty-seven years, paced behind the desk in the Oval Office.

"What do we know?" the president said.

Jones didn't need to consult any notes. As news of the El Paso situation spread, information began trickling in, some from the local cops, more information from the one person not in the warehouse at the time of the attack.

"Rosanna Morales, the medical officer on site, was off today. She says a chopper landed in the parking lot. A few minutes later, the chopper left. Then the building exploded. In between there was a loud firefight."

"Any video footage of the raid? Traffic cameras with a view? Anything?"

"Not that we're aware of so far, sir."

General Jones sat with his legs crossed and his hands in his lap as bright sunshine filtered into the Oval

Medina's room at the Hamilton was as clean and comfortable as expected, just enough flash, and on the upper floors well above street level so the room was also quiet.

He unpacked carefully with the television news on, getting a sense of the local area as he listened to the news readers. After dinner delivered by room service, he showered and dressed in a very nice business casual outfit, the blue silk shirt perfectly pressed, the dark slacks perfectly creased, with polished black shoes. His tweed sport coat completed the ensemble, but the coat had an optional extra Medina had personally installed. The inner lining, near the hip, contained leather sleeves that held a set of very sharp throwing knives, two on each side. He buttoned the jacket and gave himself a once over in the bathroom mirror. No bulges showed.

He hadn't thought there would be any sign of the knives. They were flat, the handles polished smooth like the rest of the knife, the edges honed to precision. He could slice the air with those knives.

He took a cab to an upscale bar called the Executive Room and nodded at the doorman, handing him a cash tip, he the man held the door. Medina let out a low whistle. The Executive Room was very nice, lots of leather seats and bright colors, the place packed with people who actually looked worthy of spending time with; the women dressed seriously to kill and almost making their men invisible. Nowhere in the bar would one find the dregs from the street.

Quiet piano music played, thanks to the woman on

a small stage in front of the piano. She wore a black sequined dress and the sequins sparked under the stage lights.

Medina found a spot at the bar and ordered a gin and tonic with a slice of lime. He leaned against the rail and watched the activity around him and took his time with the drink. There was no rush. Not tonight.

Medina finished his gin and tonic and turned back to the bar. The female bartender noticed and asked if he wanted a refill. Medina said no. He said he wanted to see Mr. Price. The woman frowned.

"There's nobody named Price working here."

Medina spoke carefully. "Yes, there is. Tell him A Z sent me."

"A Z?"

"Do I need to speak slower?"

The woman ignored the crack as she filled another order. Medina kept his eyes on her, and she must have felt the stare, because presently she pulled a telephone from beneath the bar and pressed the "o" button.

She turned her back to the customers as she spoke, keeping her head down and voice low, but she was looking at Medina's reflection in the mirror. He was looking at her looking at him.

She hung up and phone and leaned across the bar to him.

"Turn around. Do not leave your spot. There are three guys watching you and they all have automatic weapons."

Medina shrugged. "That's fine."

She moved on quickly, passing behind her male partner, helping customers at the far end of the bar.

Medina turned and leaned back again. The couple

CHAPTER 18

TWO MEN INSIDE.

One stood behind a table with a variety of open zipper cases displaying handguns, submachine guns, and explosive devices.

Medina glanced at the second man. Bodyguard. He stood off to the side of the dimly lit room with his hands linked in front of him.

The man behind the table said, "I wasn't expecting you to show up."

"Who else would be here?"

The man shrugged. "Somebody else to do your errands while you hide out."

"I like to be in front of things," *El Cortador* said.

The man behind the table, wearing a dark suit, his bald head and goatee visible in the low light above, waved his hands over the table display.

"Various items for you to consider."

Medina stepped close. He unbuttoned his tweed coat.

He wasn't terribly interested in the auto loading pistols. What caught Medina's eye was the short-barreled submachine gun in the middle zipper case, with a folding stock, and a barrel less than eight inches. Easy to hide under a coat. The gun seller pointed out they accepted magazines with capacities between 10 and 30 rounds. The other weapon in the middle case was the latest and greatest from the U.S. military inventory, a Heckler & Koch M320 breech-loading grenade launcher. Five explosive projectiles for the launcher were also in the case. Much like the M-79 of the Vietnam era and the later M203 which mounted under the barrel of the M-16 rifle, the HK M320 could be used as a weapon itself, or attached under a rifle or carbine such as the M-16, the M-4, or the short-barreled submachine gun it shared a case with. Medina said he'd take both weapons. And the case of explosives.

"Is the cartel paying or did you bring cash?"

Median smiled and snaked a hand under his coat. He had his orders. There were to be no loose ends, no potential for blowback.

The gun seller smiled.

The blade flashed in Medina's hands, and before the bodyguard could move hand to coat, Medina had pivoted to face him. The knife left his hand in a blur, burying itself the in the bodyguard's neck.

The gun seller let out a yell cut short by another flash of steel. Another shot straight through the throat.

The door opened.

Medina's third knife missed the escort's neck, landing instead in the upper chest. As the man grabbed at the smooth hilt, Medina rushed forward with another knife in hand, slashing the man's throat, stepping back as a flood of red splashed on the floor.

Medina grabbed the two zipper cases, closing them quickly, slinging one over his back and holding the other.

He exited the way he came in. Nobody noticed him or what he was carrying; if they did, they made no obvious signs.

Medina did glance at the bar before he left.

One last look at the female bartender.

She'd seen him up close.

He'd deal with her later.

———

Mexico City, Police Airfield

John Kane found Captain Rico Ramirez standing outside the main building of the police airfield, staring off into the distance beyond the control tower at the opposite edge of the runways. It was quite the view, jagged mountains scratching the blue sky, wide open plains. It was the kind of view you could get lost in and Kane said so as he stopped beside the Mexican drug cop.

"Any word on your people?" Kane said.

Ramirez's team had moved on from the airfield, taking collected information back to their headquarters. The wounded were moved to various hospitals. Because Team Reaper had no com link to El Paso and could make no arrangements for extraction, Rico was "babysitting" the team until arrangements were made.

Like Kane, he wore street clothes, with a pistol on his hip.

Kane had added his web gear to his tee-shirt and jeans, his HK 416 slung across his back. Because he didn't know what was happening, and had heard no follow-up from General Jones, he wanted to be ready for anything. His team were within arm's length of their weapons at all times as well.

The small skeleton crew at the airfield didn't seem to mind the Americans being there, though. It brought the field more activity than they usually saw.

Axe Burton certainly didn't mind. One of the ladies on the day crew, a woman named Leticia, had his attention, and seemed to be warming up to Team Reaper's resident ladies' man.

"The wounded are doing okay; some were moved to intensive care after surgery," Ramirez said. "They'll fight another day."

"And the intel you brought back?"

Ramirez shrugged. "It will take weeks to sort through."

"Think you got what you needed?"

Ramirez turned his gaze from the horizon to smile at Kane. "Oh, yes. Tenfold. We'll wrap up what's left of *el-Jefe's* cartel without breaking a sweat."

Kane laughed. "We always say that. We always sweat more than we think."

Ramirez frowned and looked to the north, following the parallel lines of the runway. Two dots in the distance. Growing larger.

Kane said, "Are we expecting company?"

"No."

Ramirez ran into the main building to consult the air traffic crew.

Kane ran to the makeshift barracks to alert his people.

They were under attack.

This wasn't random. It was coordinated. Something bad happened in El Paso; he realized now he might be cut off from Team Bravo forever. And now Team Reaper was also being targeted. It meant only one thing.

Somebody high on the food chain had betrayed them.

———

Valdo Mendez had more firepower this time, and a renewed commitment to accomplish his mission.

He had no intention of going back to Banderas and Zamorano to say he had failed.

They'd paid him a lot of money, after all. He had to deliver results or risk his reputation. And his life.

This time, Team Reaper wouldn't simply *walk* away.

Sitting in the passenger seat of the attack chopper, a wider variety of weapon systems at the touch of his fingers, he watched the airfield increase in size as they approached. Once again, Mendez would handle air support while a detachment of cartel-hired mercenaries handled the fight on the ground.

His helicopter had more than a single rotary cannon. Missile pods on either side, and a second rotary cannon on the pilot's side of the chopper.

Mendez brimmed with anticipation. The kill was in sight.

A female's voice, from the control tower, came over the radio. She demanded to know who they were and what they were doing near a restricted area.

Mendez told the pilot not to respond.

CHAPTER 19

MENDEZ FLICKED SELECTOR switches on the console in front of him, shouting into his radio for the ground troops to descend while he provided covering fire.

The fire control stick stood between his knees, his hand wrapped lovingly around the control as he waited for a light on the console to turn from green to red, indicating that the rocket pods were warmed up and ready to fire.

He motioned the pilot to turn left. The pilot did. The control tower loomed ahead, the female controller's voice still demanding answers, Mendez laughing as he pressed the trigger on his control stick.

Rockets flashed from the right-side pod, closing the gap between chopper and control tower in seconds. The top of the building, the circular, glass-enclosed control room, exploded in a bright fireball, debris raining onto the ground.

The pilot swung right. Mendez fired more rockets,

the remaining salvo in the right-side pod, and then the left pod. Larger buildings below exploded, the pilot then dropping low and closing in on a hangar filled with helicopters. Mendez worked the twin rotary cannons next, hosing the building and helicopters with steel-core projectiles that ripped through metal, steel and glass and left destruction in its wake.

The pilot pulled up, going into a sweeping turn around the airfield.

Mendez watched the second chopper touch down and his mercenary team pile out.

A response team was already gathering to fight back. Mendez smiled. Team Reaper itself. He told the pilot to head for them, and tapped his index finger on the trigger of his fire control.

———

Minutes before, Axe Burton and Leticia Chavez were chatting at her work station, each with a hot coffee, Axe asking questions about the radar units the airport used, and how much air traffic they actually saw. She told him it depended on how many government and police airplanes were in the air and passing through; the rest of the time they warned off stray aircraft that wandered into their restricted air space.

She was a soft-spoken woman with dark hair and eyes and one of the most attractive smiles Axe had ever seen. He kept using bad jokes on her to get her to laugh, and it worked every time. Ignoring chastising eyes from the control tower supervisor nearby, Axe kept up the banter and chat, until blips on the radar put Leticia back into work mode.

The blips on the radar had wandered into the restricted area.

Leticia Chavez tried to raise the incoming aircraft on the radio but they did not respond.

The air control supervisor wandered over and she updated him. The blips kept moving across the screen. Axe, his rifle strapped behind his back, wearing his full web gear like the rest of the team, grabbed a pair of binoculars from a table and went to the right side of the tower, peering through the windows at the incoming aircraft.

"Two choppers," he reported. "Heavily armed."

Axe raised Kane on the radio.

"We see them," Reaper One said. "You better get down here."

"Copy."

Axe said goodbye to Leticia and her supervisor and started down the steps leading to the ground.

He was halfway out the door and stepping across dried grass when the lead chopper opened fire with rockets, and the tower control room above erupted in flames.

He yelled as hot debris landed around him, some pieces striking his bare arms and neck. He hunkered close to the base of the building, and he didn't need to look up. He knew Leticia and her supervisor were dead. The chopper with the guns swooped across the field. Axe unslung his HK 416 and tried to get a bead on the cockpit bubble, but the chopper moved too fast. It hosed the hangar containing other choppers. Axe worked his way around the building and finally lined up the chopper in the HK's sights, but his trio of single shots appeared to do nothing to the flying machine as it climbed and made a long right turn.

"Reaper Four, where are you?"

Kane on the radio.

"Tower, Reaper One. Made it out just in time."

"Look right."

Axe looked, leading with the HK, as the second chopper touched down. Side doors opened and men armed to the teeth rushed out onto the field.

Axe dropped to one knee to steady his aim and make himself a small target for return fire. He lined up front and rear sight and worked the trigger, spacing out his rounds, the HK kicking lightly against his shoulder.

Two of the attackers dropped to the 5.56mm death blasts before the group fired back, Axe dropping flat as bullets smacked the base of the tower behind him.

He breathed slowly, nerves steady, and kept firing, dropping back to change mags and engage again. By then, the gunners were running across the field, the chopper lifting off. Axe focused on the helicopter. He flicked the HK's selector to full auto, aimed for the cockpit, and let the weapon rip in controlled bursts.

He was rewarded with splintering plexiglass and a spray of red on the other side, the pilot's body slumping forward, the chopper's nose dipping. It continued moving forward for a moment, then the nose touched the ground. The chopper flipped over, tail rising skyward, and came down on rotors churning the grass before exploding.

Axe made himself as flat as possible. A heat wave washed over him. No chopper parts nicked him, but he heard the pieces landing nearby.

He looked up. The gun crew was engaging Kane and the others near the makeshift barracks and the burning main building.

He had no idea who these attackers were, but they'd killed too many people already.

CHAPTER 20

JOHN "REAPER" Kane shouted to Brick and Arenas, "Spread out! Try and get 'em in a crossfire!"

To Cara: "Roof of the hangar!"

"You mean what's left of it?"

"You're a sniper and it's the only high ground I can think of right now! Go!"

Cara didn't argue. She ran, the HK sniper rifle clutched close to her chest. The hangar wasn't on fire, but the cannon fire damage, with big holes in the walls and choppers, made it obvious that area was otherwise useless except for a sniper's nest.

Kane and Rico Ramirez stayed close to the main building, at a corner not on fire, well away of the hot flames behind them and burning embers that drifted down from above.

"Do we have any vehicles?" Kane said.

"Land Rovers in back."

"Check on 'em. Stay on coms."

"Copy."

Ramirez bolted for the rear of the building, leaving Kane alone.

Automatic weapons fire crackled across the airfield as Team Reaper engaged the newly arrived force crossing the runway. His eye was on the son of a bitch in the chopper that kept making circles over the airfield, probably itching for another chance to use his rotary cannons.

Kane shouldered his carbine and opened fire, aiming ahead of the helicopter, sparks on the body indicating where his rounds struck. He lifted his muzzle and let off a short full-auto burst as the chopper steered in his direction. Kane ran in the direction Ramirez had gone, slapping a fresh mag into the weapon. He held up his right arm as a shield from the heat of the burning building on his right, staying close to the makeshift barracks on the left, where fallen embers had ignited the roof.

The chopper's cannons opened fire, Kane running closer to the burning building, the swarm of slugs smacking the ground around him as the billowing smoke blocked the chopper gunner's aim.

"Comin' to you, Rico!" Kane shouted into his com unit.

"I see you, Reaper One!"

Kane coughed as the thick smoke made his eyes itch but the chopper flew overhead, ahead of him, Kane cutting left for a small garage where Rico Ramirez waved him down. The Mexican federal cop stood in front of a Land Rover with its engine running.

"Hop in!" Ramirez said.

"Where are we going?"

"Hangar with the helicopters. They might be toast

but we can grab one of the mounted .50-calibers and use that against our friend up there. Your HK won't cut it."

"You're telling me!"

Kane jumped into the passenger side of the Land Rover. Ramirez put the vehicle in gear and left a patch of rubber on the cement as he pulled out.

———

Cara ignored the gunfire behind her. Her eyes remained focused on the hangar where the damaged helicopters sat, and the ladder on the side of the building used by maintenance crews to maintain the building.

The shooting behind her was intense. But none of the rounds came her way.

She was aware of the chopper flying overhead, and the fusillade of cannon fire seconds ago, but the pilot of that bird was also ignoring her.

She reached the ladder, using one hand and both feet to scale the height. She clutched the HK sniper rifle in her right hand. Reaching the roof, grateful for the flat area, she set up on the edge, jacking a round into the chamber and lowering the front bipod.

She filled her sight with the enemy. They were advancing slowly, trading fire with Brick and Arenas, but not yet within any type of crossfire the two Reaper warriors might have arranged. The burning wreck behind them offered Cara mild encouragement that they might make it out of this skirmish long enough to figure out what the hell was happening, not only in Mexico, but in El Paso.

She fired. One trooper dropped. Another tripped over him, Cara putting a round in the man's head as he tried to rise.

She shifted her aim. Fired. Missed. Fired again. Another miss as the troopers advanced.

She took a deep breath, relaxed her trigger finger a moment, and then resumed.

One shot; one more down. She barely felt the recoil as each projectile left the barrel.

Sweat dripping into her eye blurred her telescope view. She pulled away long enough to wipe her face, put her eye back to the scope, and looked for another target.

———

Valdo Mendez watched the speeding Land Rover, with a frown of curiosity.

They pair weren't speeding away, they were heading into the fight, back down the space between the burning main building and its smoldering neighbor, but they weren't stopping to pick up comrades.

By the time the Rover screeched right and headed for the helicopter hangar he'd hosed earlier, he figured out the plan.

They wanted the high-powered weapons stored in the hangar.

Should have used the rockets on the hangar.

Mendez directed the pilot as he wrapped his hand around the firing control once again. He was out of rockets, but still had plenty of steel-core ammo left in the rotary guns.

Then he saw the woman on the roof. Sunlight flashed off her sniper scope.

"Pull up!"

The sniper's rifle flashed once.

The bullet punched through the Plexiglas in front of the pilot and punctured the pilot's left eye. Without uttering a sound, the pilot slumped forward, his weight falling against the controls.

Mendez tried to move the body, but couldn't get leverage from his position. He tried to grab the controls, the chopper weaving left and right and then left and down.

———

Kane watched the chopper chase them, in the passenger side mirror. Then he looked ahead and watched Cara's sniper rifle flash once. He laughed. *Maybe we won't need the .50.*

"What's so funny?"

"Look behind us."

The chopper weaved back and forth, finally pitching left and diving headlong into the runway. The shock of the explosion lifted the back end of the Land Rover, Kane grabbing onto a side handle to steady himself.

Rico Ramirez screeched to a halt outside the hangar.

Both men climbed out, Kane aware of the cease in shooting, Cara shouting, "Got him!" as she rushed down the maintenance ladder, a big grin on her face and a big rifle in both hands.

"Bullseye," Kane said. He and Rico turned to look

at the second burning chopper. "But we still have no answers," he added.

Brick and Arenas and Axe checked in over the com unit, reporting that the attack force was down and they were looking for survivors.

"They won't have any answers for us," Kane said.

He turned to Rico and Cara.

"The only answers we're going to get will come from General Jones."

Rico Ramirez nodded. Cara said nothing.

CHAPTER 21

El Paso, TX, Foundation Surgical Hospital

GENERAL HANK JONES wore civilian clothes as he walked through the automatic sliding doors of Foundation Surgical Hospital. A consultation with the directory, and a question from a passing nurse or two, directed him to the floor where Team Bravo had been secured.

Jones recognized several U.S. Marshals standing guard as he stepped onto the floor. They were there at the order of the president, who wanted Team Bravo watched over because President Carter did not believe what had happened was a random retaliatory strike by an unknown cartel. Something else was at play.

He hoped Kane and his crew were safe in Mexico until they figured out what was happening, or at least figured out how to get them back into the U.S. to a secure location.

He identified himself to one of the marshals, who

introduced him to the shift supervisor, who checked the general's identification and confirmed with Washington that he was supposed to be present. The supervisor then brought General Jones to a Hispanic woman in her 30s whom Jones had never met, but recognized from file photos.

She wasn't sitting in the waiting area, or chatting with the nurses at the circular desk near the elevator. She was pacing the room, arms folded, pensive. Her suspicious eyes landed hard on Jones as he approached.

"Doctor Morales?" the general said before the marshal introduced them.

She nodded; the marshal departed.

Her dark hair was tied back, her brown eyes sizing him up. He was taller than her. She had to look up to meet his gaze.

"We haven't met. I'm Hank Jones."

"I know who you are, General Jones."

The general had no time for her aloofness, but this also wasn't the time to tell her so. She was probably more concerned for the Bravo crew than the surgeons in the building.

"I need to know what happened, Doctor."

She shook her head. "All I know is what Brooke told me."

"Brooke Reynolds?"

"She's the only one able to talk."

"The only—"

"Everybody else is messed up pretty bad, General. Brooke only suffered a concussion because Sam Swift jumped on top of her before a grenade went off. He saved her life, but nearly lost his own.

"The surgeons pulled several chunks of shrapnel out of Pete Traynor's backside, and he'd been shot too.

"General Thurston was shot twice in the chest. Pete Teller suffered injuries from the grenade blast.

"Luis Ferrero was also shot twice, but he managed to get out of the building to tell the emergency units on scene that there were others inside."

General Hank Jones had no words. He only blinked.

"Where were you?" he finally said.

She scoffed. "Day off. When Team Reaper is in the field there isn't much for me to do."

"Prognosis? Is there any good news?"

"Nobody's going to die. So far. Everybody but Brooke is in intensive care, hooked up to oxygen and IV drips. They're hurt bad. These aren't those silly flesh wounds that never seem to hurt anybody, General."

Jones nodded. He didn't need to be reminded of the horrors of combat. He'd lost plenty of friends to enemy fire and, worse, some to genuine training mishaps that shouldn't have happened and certainly shouldn't have ended lives.

He asked Rosanna Morales to follow him away from the hub of the nurse's station and the watching eyes of the U.S. Marshals. They moved to a hallway, the closed doors of hospital rooms only feet from them. He spoke quietly, almost a whisper.

"Doctor Morales, I'm going to need your help. The president ordered the marshals here, and my people are also getting together to plan the biggest cover up this city has ever seen. I'm going to need help keeping their families out of the picture until we figure out what happened."

"And create a story in case the worst happens?"

"Exactly."

"You'll never pull it off."

"Doctor—"

"Ever hear of Reddit? Every two-bit conspiracy nut on the internet is going to be talking about what happened at that warehouse."

"We don't have a *choice*, Doctor. You need to help me. You need to help *me* help *them*. This isn't about what anybody else thinks."

She nodded. "All right."

"I have your word?"

"Anything you need."

General Jones let out a sigh of relief. She might be distant, but he could count on her.

"Now, part two," he said. "Where is John Kane and the rest of Team Reaper?"

"Mission in Mexico," she said. "They were working with the federal drug task force. I haven't spoken to any of them since they left."

"*Where* in Mexico, Doctor? Kane called me when he couldn't reach Thurston."

"I don't know *where* they are, General."

Jones said, "With Bravo out of commission, they're stuck in Mexico until we can figure out how to get them out."

"Shouldn't be hard."

"Under normal circumstances, no. This isn't normal. We're under attack. And right now, keeping Team Reaper in the field might be the safest place for them to be."

She shrugged. Operations was not her specialty.

She made her contribution by keeping the bodies in one piece.

Speaking of which...

"Can I see Brooke?"

Doctor Morales nodded. "Follow me."

She led General Jones further down the hall.

CHAPTER 22

THEY FOUND Brooke Reynolds asleep in her bed, the covers pulled up to her neck. She was on her back, the upper portion of the bed raised, her head leaning to the right.

The blinds over the window had been closed, but sunlight still broke through, creating rows of shadows on the bed and floor.

Rosanna Morales gently shook Brooke awake.

The UAV pilot awoke slowly, her eyes adjusting to the sight of Morales, then shifting to General Hank Jones. Like the doctor, she had long black hair. Unlike the doctor's, Brooke's hair was a mess on the pillow.

She stared blankly, only laying back at Morales' urging. She breathed slowly.

"You're going to be okay, Brooke," the general said. "But I need you to fill in a few details of what happened."

"I'll try and remember," Brooke said.

Jones' cell phone began to ring. He said, "Excuse me," and turned away from the bed to answer.

"Jones speaking."

"General," a man on the other end said, "please hold for President Carter."

A moment later, the president said, "Hank, are you watching TV?"

"No, sir, I'm with one of Team Bravo who survived the attack."

"Turn on the news, Hank. Cable if you can. Fox or CNN."

General Jones asked for the TV remote, which Morales grabbed from Brooke's nightstand.

The TV hung on the wall ahead of the bed. Jones turned on the set, and switched channels until he found Fox.

He frowned. It wasn't what he expected, another disaster, but instead a press conference from the new president of Mexico addressing the drug war.

"Find it?" the president said.

"I see it, sir."

"You're not going to believe the words coming out of his mouth, Hank."

———

Mexico City

Mexican President Lucio Rojo, his white hair cut closer to his scalp than usual, smiled weakly at the reporters gathered in the room. He stood above them on the stage, behind a podium, but even with the seal of the president's office adorning the front of the podium, Rojo felt no protection from the horde and their inevitable questions about his change in "drug war" policy.

He didn't like conflict. He was ending the drug war to end conflict, but also inadvertently starting a new one, except his new enemies didn't use machine guns and car bombs to silence the opposition.

Fighting with words was much easier than guns.

Plus, he'd already made promises to the cartels. If he went back on his word because of a bunch of reporters acting like hyenas, he might find one of those car bombs under the presidential limousine.

Check that. I wouldn't know it was there until it exploded.

Rojo cleared his throat and the mass of journalists fell silent, their attention focused on their elected leader.

"Our nation has reached a turning point," Rojo began. He had a sheet of notes in front of him in case his memory failed under the pressure of being stared at.

"For too many years, the drug war has cost our nation millions of dollars, and claimed almost as many lives."

They might dispute that later but who cares?

"When I ran for president, I promised Mexico peace. I intend to keep that promise. I am here to announce today an end to the drug war."

Gasps and murmurs from the horde.

Rojo swallowed and pressed on.

"We will withdraw the military from the streets, police forces will be re-organized, with less emphasis on paramilitary activity. We are not legalizing drugs. There will still be work for our law enforcement professionals to do, but we are no longer going about this with violence as our first option."

Rojo paused a moment, and was about to continue

when the questions started, the group of reporters shouting over each other to be heard, cameras flashing, television cameras recording, all of it overloading Rojo's senses. He blinked a few times, looked away to take a deep breath, re-center himself.

The questions didn't stop.

So much for my speech.

He glanced to his right. From the wings, Federico Esteves urged him on with a thumbs up, mouthing, "Keep going."

Rojo held up his hands.

"I will take no questions now. Please quiet down. No questions. There will be plenty of time for questions when I have finished my statement. Please."

It took a few minutes, and more urging from the president, but eventually the reporters settled down.

Rojo took a deep breath and continued.

El Paso, TX

"Can you believe that load of shit?"

General Hank Jones didn't stifle a laugh. President Jack Carter could be quite blunt sometimes.

"I don't know how he's going to pull it off, sir, even with the explanation he's giving right now."

"What's your first reaction?"

Jones glanced at Brooke Reynolds and Dr. Morales, both of whom were fixed on the television.

"I'm beginning to put two and two together, Mister President."

"You think he made a deal with the cartels?"

"He had to. If he wants them to stop the killing, they needed something to make it worth their while."

"Team Reaper?"

"Exactly, Mister President."

"We need to get them out of Mexico. Do you have an extraction plan in mind?"

"We're going to need to develop one."

"Get it done. And then I want them to stay in the field."

"I've thought keeping them moving might be best, sir."

"We have a problem brewing in New Mexico," the president said. "I want them there to check it out."

"I'm not aware of the issues in New Mexico, sir."

"When you meet with your aids, they will have the data. You can pass it along to Kane."

"Will do, sir."

"All right, Hank, take care."

The president rang off and General Jones put away his phone. He turned back to Brooke and Morales. The footage from Mexico, and his whirlwind chat with the president, left him breathless. He looked at the two women and tried to think of something to say.

CHAPTER 23

Mexico City

JOHN KANE SAT in his hotel room and cleaned his guns

After the fight at the airfield, Rico had arranged with his department to relocate Team Reaper to a hotel in Mexico City where they could lay low until they heard from General Jones.

He sat in the complimentary bathrobe, his hair still wet from his shower, grateful to get the desert dust off his skin, but his lack of fresh clothes posed a problem. He had only two sets of street clothes, and his second set was on the bed waiting for him.

Still no word from Jones.

And the press conference put on by President Rojo had sent a chill up his spine. He *really* needed to talk to Jones.

The sat phone sat on the table to his left in case the general found the time to reach out.

He'd ordered everybody to settle in their rooms and

get some rest, but he doubted they were resting any more than he was.

As he scrubbed the receiver of the SIG M-17, the sat phone rang.

Kane let it ring twice as he put his disassembled weapon on the table, then picked up the phone. He knew better than to answer gruffly. He said, "Yes, sir."

"Is your team safe?"

"We're at a hotel, General. Rico Ramirez arranged it."

"I need you out of there ASAP."

"Are we walking?"

"I'm arranging a flight through the CIA since they have jets in your area. A private plane will meet you at the southern-most hangar at Mexico City Airport. Are you writing this down?"

"One moment, sir." Kane grabbed a hotel notepad and pen from the nightstand. "Go."

General Jones gave Kane a rundown of the extraction plan. He didn't want Kane to contact Ramirez or anybody else in the Mexican government. He only wanted Team Reaper to depart the hotel and get to the airport by any means available.

"The plane will take you to New Mexico, where we have another problem."

"Wait, what about El Paso?" Kane said.

"We'll get to that in a minute."

Kane's pulse quickened. *Why is he stalling?*

"Both the president and myself think you and your people will be safer if you remain in the field."

"What do you mean *safer*?"

"Been watching the news?"

"You mean the Mexican president? I can't believe my ears."

"Neither could I or President Carter. We think Rojo has made a deal with the cartels to stop the drug war, but it means delivering Team Reaper on a platter. Starting with El Paso. It's the only thing that makes sense."

Kane gripped the sat phone a little tighter.

Starting with El Paso?

But he didn't push General Jones for more. Jones would get to that update in a moment.

If Kane could stand to wait.

"That explains what happened to us," Kane said instead, and told Jones of the attack choppers showing up at *el-Jefe's* mansion and the airfield. "They weren't part of el-Jefe's group at all."

"I don't think so. You're lucky you all made it out of there."

"We're pretty beat, sir. If you want us to continue into New Mexico, we're low on ammo. Another fight—"

"I will have contacts in Alamogordo provide everything you need," the general said. "We have an open border there, Reaper. The leak needs to be plugged. You'll get full details when you land. The sheriff you'll be working with served with me in the Rangers."

"Understood. Now tell me about headquarters."

Jones let out a sigh. Kane braced for the worst. He sat on the floor against the bed as Jones provided every detail he could, Kane's heart sinking, dreading the idea of having to pass the information along to the rest of the team.

"Prognosis?" Kane said when General Jones finished. His voice broke a little. He cleared his throat.

"They're stable, but still in intensive care."

"What about security?"

"The president assigned a team of US Marshals to keep an eye on Bravo."

"You sure they're going to be okay?"

"I said they're *stable*, Reaper. I don't know about okay. The only one not hurt terribly is Brooke Reynolds. Doctor Morales wasn't there at the time. All of my information comes from them."

Kane closed his eyes. "Okay. Thank you, sir."

"I don't envy you talking to the others."

"I don't either."

"It's the hardest part of being in command, Reaper. Trust me."

"I don't doubt it, sir."

"Just make sure you and your crew are on that jet."

Kane laughed. "A CIA escort home will be a first for us."

The two men said goodbye. Kane sat against the bed a moment longer, staring at the carpet.

The only way to break the news to the others was to be blunt and to the point.

He used the hotel phone on the nightstand to call each member one by one and ask them to report to his room pronto.

Alamogordo, New Mexico

Vartan "Vic" Nazarian locked his office. The night crew had replaced the daytime crew, and he spoke to the deputies for a few moments. Most were going out on patrol; others remained at the station to cover their various investigations. Nazarian normally knew a little about what each deputy was doing, but he had bigger matters on his mind tonight.

Like setting up a death squad and keeping it a secret from the people closest to me.

He climbed into his truck and drove out of the city, into the desert, pulling off the roadway at an abandoned gas station. He stopped the truck. The old pumps were deteriorating; the roof of the station itself sagging, but the owner refused to sell the property or rebuild the station. He had opened other gas stations further along, bigger ones with fast food outlets attached, but his original location remained a wreck.

Nazarian rolled down his window and shut off the truck.

He was early.

Then the light flashed in his face.

CHAPTER 24

"YOU'RE EARLY," said the arrival.

"For the same reason as you," Nazarian said.

The light switched off. Nazarian was left with ruined night vision and a spot in front of his retina. He closed his eyes a moment.

"Sorry, Vic," the other man said. "Had to be sure."

Nazarian opened his eyes. He could see again. "Your crew under surveillance?"

"We always assume. You should have seen the dirty looks I got when I told them I was meeting the sheriff. Come on, let's talk."

Nazarian exited his truck. He shut the door quietly.

He followed Roger Cross into the dilapidated gas station. They made their way to a back room where tables and chairs had been set up, a coffee maker in one corner that was too new to be a permanent resident. No other clutter to speak of, though the room smelled of dust, and layers of dust existed here and there. No decorations. Nothing to indicate it was used regularly by the

New Mexico Militia for clandestine chats. Cross commanded the Otero County battalion.

Nazarian didn't consider state militias as overgrown boy scouts or overweight incels trying to play army. He knew men like Cross took the role of civil defense seriously, while at the same time being a forever resident on the "usual suspects" list.

It was a "cross" that Roger Cross and his crew accepted because they knew they weren't the enemy. The security of the United States was important to them, as was the well-being of New Mexico citizens. During fires, floods, or other disasters, Nazarian had been impressed with the Otero County militia stepping up to help and assist in areas the National Guard and other emergency units had yet to reach.

Nazarian figured the battalion would be interested in his anti-drug proposal. They fired a lot of guns, practiced military drills, and spoke of the possibility of having to fight a tyrannical government, so they at least knew how to handle themselves. Shooting targets in the middle of the desert, however, was far different from engaging real humans who fired back.

And knew a few awful tricks of their own.

Nazarian truly wasn't sure they'd be interested in the fight, but he had no other ideas. He needed men with guns who had the ability to use them well. The militia seemed like the best place to start.

Nobody would ever accuse Nazarian of going "by the book".

Cross moved to the coffee maker and poured into two Styrofoam cups. He handed one to Nazarian.

"Still like it black?"

"You remembered," the sheriff said.

"You've done us a few favors, Sheriff. We appreciate you."

"Then why the dirty looks?"

Cross shrugged. "Some people will always be suspicious."

They sat down. Cross wiped dust off the table with a handkerchief from his back pocket. The chair Nazarian used wobbled a little.

"I'm hoping you can help me again," the sheriff said. "This is a very unusual request, and everything we talk about tonight, if you tell me no, must remain confidential."

"Wow. You have my attention. What's on your mind?"

Roger Cross had close-cropped dark hair and a tan. Gentle eyes. He was a veterinarian, of high regard in town, in his professional life.

"We have a serious problem at the border."

"The check-points are closed, yeah. We've been thinking of rotating a few teams through the area."

Good. He's already halfway where I need him.

"It's bigger than that," Nazarian said. "The cartels are taking advantage of the gap, among other things, to get drugs into the US through New Mexico. The feds are aware of the problem, but solving the problem isn't on the priority list right now."

"Not with that prick Carter in charge, no."

Nazarian sipped his coffee. He wasn't here to argue politics. He let the comment pass.

"You heard about that couple killed the other night?" he said instead.

"Yeah. Is it true they had a shoot-out with druggies?"

Nazarian nodded. "They did well, got one of the guys, but they were both killed."

"Manage to track down the wounded guy?"

"We tried all the doctors we knew of who had done favors for the cartels in the past, but the guy didn't turn up, and we haven't had any reports of anybody discovering stray bodies, either."

Nazarian bit back further frustration. The efforts of his crew had been fruitless indeed, and that hurt. It meant the cartels had changed their method of operations. It meant his deputies were once again playing catch-up with an opponent who always remained one step ahead.

"Maybe he wasn't as hurt as the evidence suggested."

"Who knows? All I know is I have two dead citizens, drug thugs on the loose, not enough deputies, and a federal government more concerned with illegals in California than drug thugs in New Mexico."

"Sounds about right." Cross drank some coffee.

And now Nazarian was at the point of officially proposing his idea. Instead, he froze.

"Spit it out, Sheriff," Cross said. "What are you asking of the New Mexico Citizens Militia?"

"We need shooters at the border."

"Whoa."

"I mean roving patrols, like you said, to intercept the drug shipments and deal with them."

"Hey, Sheriff, that's a little out of our—"

"Really, Roger? We're being invaded. This is *exactly* in our wheelhouse."

Roger Cross made circles with his coffee cup. "You plan for it but you never think it will really happen."

"I know a lot of dead cops who said the same thing."

Cross looked up sharply. Nazarian met his gaze.

CHAPTER 25

THE KIND EYES of Roger Cross looked grim now. "What you're proposing—"

"You're going to need to make it clear to your people that they are volunteers, they are risking their lives, their freedom, their livelihood, possibly creating problems at home—"

"Jesus, you make it sound so exciting."

"It's not a game, Roger."

"I *know* that, Sheriff."

"Hey—"

Cross held up both hands in mock surrender. "My apologies, Sheriff." He put his hands down and leaned forward. "I appreciate the position you're in. I can take this to my men, but the problem is some of them are going to think it's a trap."

"What would help convince them otherwise?"

"They'll need a heck of a lot more than my word."

"I'll be happy to address them myself, tell them the same thing I've told you."

"In front of more witnesses?"

"In front of more witnesses. They need to know my neck is on the line, too. Maybe then we can reach an agreement."

"I can't promise I can deliver a lot of people," Cross said.

"The ones I want are the combat vets, men not afraid to kill, aware of the risks."

"I got a few of those."

"Why don't you get them together, and tell me where you want me to be, and we can all talk it out."

Cross laughed. "I can already hear them asking if this is a set-up."

"If it is, I ain't hiding anything. I'm wearing my uniform and badge right now, aren't I?"

"You sure are." Cross laughed. "You're crazy, Sheriff."

"If by crazy you mean tired of not being able to protect my county, then yeah, I'm crazy."

"Vic, let's be real for a minute."

"Okay."

"If I'm going to take this to the guys, they have to know, and maybe I do too, that there isn't any other way. The Feds can change their mind tomorrow, you know."

"They won't. I don't think we can wait. You'll have the cooperation of my office. I'll do anything necessary to keep the backfire away from you so if and when the Feds get their shit together, your team can fade away."

Cross laughed a little. "What did so-and-so say about being the one to count the votes?"

"Exactly."

Cross nodded.

Nazarian downed the rest of his drink and stood up. "Thanks for the coffee."

Cross left his chair as well. "I'll walk you out."

———

Nazarian loosened his grip on the steering wheel of his truck. He kept tensing his grip and causing an ache in his wrist. His conversation with Cross weighed on him in ways he didn't think he'd experience. He'd never been one to flagrantly break the law, yet here he was conspiring to do so, and no amount of justification seemed to make the weight go away.

But he also couldn't simply sit and let the invasion continue. Until Washington shifted into gear, he needed a vigilante force. It was an idea about 150 years too late for the new era, but his frontier predecessors certainly would have agreed with him.

He watched the city lights as the engine droned and the truck neared the edge of the city. He wanted to get back to normal civilization and fast. He needed a drink.

His cell rang. He fished the phone from his jacket pocket, expecting to see Roger Cross' name on the display, but instead a number he didn't recognize. Nazarian was about to put the phone back and let voicemail take the call when instinct took hold. He needed the answer. He pressed the green button to pick up and held the phone to his ear.

"Nazarian," he said.

"Sheriff? This is General Hank Jones, Chairman of the Joint Chiefs in Washington."

"You don't have to remind me, General, I took your orders for years."

Nazarian had been a Staff Sergeant under *Colonel* Hank Jones' command in the 75th Rangers. Hearing the old man's voice was a nice distraction to what was on his mind, and unusual enough for him to wonder why Jones was calling.

"Just as I had hoped, Vic. How are you?"

"Got a lot going on, sir. What can I help you with?"

"I'm calling because of what you have going on. I understand from a mutual friend at Homeland that you need some help."

Nazarian slowed his truck and pulled to the shoulder and kept his foot on the brake.

"What have you heard, General?"

"You have a problem with drug trafficking, a pair of recent murders, and a leaky border."

"It's leaking the wrong way, sir."

"I understand. Vic, I'm in command of a new team these days, anti-drug operations are their specialty, and I'd like to send them your way."

"Okay. Certainly. When are they getting here?"

"They finished a job in Mexico and are flying north right now. The squad leader is a man named John Kane. He'll get in touch with you and coordinate from there. He has four other teammates with him. Don't worry about their equipment, we have contacts in the area who will take care of them. All I want you to do is act as our liaison in Otero County, and provide your expertise when it's required."

"What's their mission, sir? Are they here to observe?"

"Oh, they'll observe."

Nazarian's voice dropped a little. "I see."

"They'll observe long enough to identify the enemy and then *roast* the sons of bitches, Vic."

Nazarian let out a laugh. "Now *that's* what I wanted to hear, sir. We are really hurting here. We need help in a big way."

"Expect my people shortly."

"Thank you for calling, General."

Jones said goodbye and rang off.

Nazarian put his phone away and let out a satisfied breath. He pulled back onto the road. The drone of the engine soothed him now; he held the wheel loosely, enjoying the ride. He was glad he had taken the call. He wondered if his arrangement with Cross, and the addition of the general's strike team, might be the exact formula required to chase the cartels out of Otero County for good.

CHAPTER 26

Mexico City

PRESIDENT LUCIO ROJO dabbed a handkerchief across his forehead.

His excuse was that he was sweating under the bright television light before him.

The truth was, he was sweating because of the hard questions the interviewer was asking.

The press conference had set off a fire storm of controversy Rojo had expected, but wasn't ready to deal with. Too many inquiries might reveal the true nature of the cessation of hostilities he now advocated.

He had agreed to let Sylvia Menendez of *TV Azteca* interview him in his office at the *Palacio Nacional* because she was young, beautiful, and not known for asking tough questions. She was the reporter who covered the easy stories, the celebrity interviews, the softball stuff.

But somebody had given her questions to ask and she wasn't afraid to bring them up.

"Mister President," she said, her dark eyes scanning an index card. "What do we do with the one hundred fifty drug kingpins currently in prison or awaiting extradition to the United States?"

She certainly looked the part of a cheesecake network news babe. Little black dress, strategically short and tight in all the right places, high heels, perfect hair and makeup. Her perfect legs were crossed almost provocatively, as if she used them as a visual distraction, a ruse to get Rojo thinking carnal thoughts while she bombed him with questions that made him inwardly squirm.

I'll never allow TV Azteca into this palace again!

Rojo cleared his throat. The bright camera light stood behind her to the left; to her right, the camera, aimed at Rojo's face, didn't move. The lone bespectacled operator behind the camera, whom Rojo barely saw because of the bright light, hovered like a specter.

This is not an interview! This is an interrogation!

"We will be in touch with our American allies," Rojo said, "to discuss alternate means of prosecution, or release."

Sylvia Menendez frowned. "You've made this decision without consulting the United States?"

"Young lady, the United *States* does not dictate the policy of *Mexico*."

She flinched, but continued. "Their contribution to the drug war—"

"I am aware of the millions and billions, young lady."

"Are we going to pay them back?"

"I cannot comment on that until our discussions begin, but I assure, and any person in the American

Office. President Carter continued to pace. His expression was twisted with thought.

"What did Morales say about casualties?"

"The Foundation Surgical Hospital reported taking in six trauma victims, but Morales hasn't been allowed access nor does she have any update on their condition."

"You sure our people were taken there?"

"She's sure."

"Who's on the way to talk to her?"

"My team. I'm the only one still in Washington."

"I need you out there, too, General."

"Yes, sir."

President Carter stopped long enough to lean on the back of his chair.

"Where is Kane and his group?"

"Mexico."

"Do they know?"

"They only know that communications have been cut off."

"Get to El Paso. I need you talking to the survivors. If there are any."

General Hank Jones didn't want to think about fatalities, but he also wasn't going to argue with the president. The situation looked grim indeed. From what he'd seen of the newspaper pictures, he was surprised anybody alive came out of that blaze.

––––––––

Dulles International Airport, Washington, D.C.

As General Jones left Washington on a private government jet, heading for El Paso, another plane landed and taxied to the terminal.

A man named Diego Medina, clutching his carry-on, holding a coat over his right arm, exited the plane and entered the terminal with the flood of other passengers. Automatically he looked for the signs directing to baggage claim—same as anybody else would.

His contact would be waiting there.

Medina walked casually. He was not a man anybody would notice. He had a strong build, but a day worker's face. He looked bored. He looked normal.

The unassuming appearance made his job easy.

Back home, in Mexico, he was known as *El Cortador*. The Cutter. His preferred method of assassination was up close, with a blade.

But on this job, he would need guns. And bombs.

The days of simple assassinations were long gone. At least he wasn't using one of those newfangled "heart attack guns" the spooks liked.

His carry-on bag contained the usual items travelers pack, in his case, a change of clothes, his blood pressure medication, a few paperback books (he didn't like e-books; he didn't like smart phones, either), and his digital music player.

Nothing out of the ordinary.

But if one had searched his wallet, one might find the usual ID cards, cash, charge cards, all that. They'd also find a folded piece of paper with a list of names, all of whom were high-ranking members of the US federal law enforcement community.

He was here to kill them one by one.

Medina traveled down an escalator to the baggage

claim area, where the carousels were already rotating, bags making their circuit. He was shorter than many people around him, and he weaved through politely to the carousel that bore his flight number.

He'd look for his contact after collecting his suitcase.

CHAPTER 17

MEDINA FOUND his contact near the exit, a driver holding a cardboard sign that read *Mr. Rufus*. Medina had no idea how the organization had come up with that name, but he acknowledged to the driver that he was Mr. Rufus, and the driver led him out of the building to a waiting car.

Medina sat in the back as the driver, without talking, pulled away from Dulles International Airport.

Medina watched the passing scenery with disinterest. He already knew the driver was taking him to his hotel, so there was no sense in asking where they were going.

Instead, Medina's thoughts turned to *the job*.

He'd carried out many murders for Victor Zamorano's cartel, and this assignment, a strike at the heart of U.S. law enforcement, would be a feather in his cap for sure. He would return to Mexico as God Among Killers.

The thought made him smile.

government who sees this, that we will work out a fair arrangement for all."

"But, Mister President—"

"Stop." Rojo leaned forward in his chair. She moved her head back a little, but remained in her seat. "I am looking out for the survival of our people. How many murders a day are there in Mexico, *young lady*? Or are you too busy interviewing soap opera stars to notice?"

"Your tone isn't necessary, sir."

"What is necessary, Sylvia, is that we solve problems. The drug problem is tearing our beautiful country apart, and I am sick of the violence."

The woman said nothing.

"If the drug war does not end, blood will flow in the streets the likes of which we have never seen. Is that what you want?"

"Mexico wants law and order, Mister President. Are the cartels now going to run unchecked in exchange for not killing anyone? How does that help Mexico and the rest of the world? Do we not have a responsibility to our global neighbors?"

Rojo ripped the lapel microphone from his shirt. "This interview is over. You will leave immediately."

Rojo left the chair and turned, walking steadily into his office. The light switched off behind him as he shut the door.

Federico Esteves waited in the office, sitting in the corner lounge area, sipping a glass of ice water.

Breathless, as if he'd completed a marathon, Rojo looked at the younger man.

"Did you listen?"

"Could have gone better, sir."

Rojo stabbed a finger at his number two. "Do *not* start with me, *pendejo*."

"Calling me stupid isn't going to help, either, sir."

Rojo huffed and dropped into the seat behind his desk, the cluttered desk, stacked with papers, responsibilities, the work of a national leader. He stared past the clutter, at the door he'd passed through.

Esteves strolled over to the desk but did not sit down. "We're going to need damage control once that interview airs."

Rojo nodded. "I am not ignorant of the consequences of my outburst, Federico."

"What worked, I think, is your insistence on the safety of Mexican citizens. That will work in our favor."

"This is going to be harder than I thought," Rojo said.

"Nothing worthwhile is easy, sir."

Rojo nodded. "We need to take a poll. See what the public thinks. They have to support the idea that their sons and daughters will not die in cartel crossfires any longer."

"I will order it done, sir."

The telephone on the right corner of Rojo's desk buzzed. The Mexican president gestured for Esteves to answer. The younger man lifted the receiver.

"Yes."

He listened, cupped the mouthpiece, and said, "The American president is on the line for you, sir."

Rojo shook his head.

"We might as well get this part out of the way," Esteves said. "It will help our response to Azteca's interview."

Rojo held out his right hand and Esteves handed him the phone.

"This is President Lucio Rojo," the man said.

"Please hold for President Carter."

The line clicked twice; then: "President Rojo?"

"President Carter. Thank you for calling. I was going to call you."

"I figured you might. I wanted to reach out first. We have some things to talk about, Mister President. Do you have some time?"

Rojo bit back a testy response. The American was toying with him and disguising it as polite diplomacy.

"I have time, Mister President," Rojo said.

"I'm wondering if you're making the right decision. Our arrangement doesn't necessarily include calling off our operations."

"I am doing what is best for my country, Mister Carter. I expect you will honor our new policy and begin withdrawing any and all units you have in Mexico."

"It's not that easy, Mister Rojo. We send you a lot of money."

"And we have appreciated your generosity. Your aid is no longer required."

Esteves winced. Rojo waved him off.

"I wish you'd reconsider."

"My decision is final, Mister Carter. My people are dying."

"People all over the world are dying because of the poison coming from your country, sir."

"Are you blaming *me*, Mister President? Are you blaming *my* country for the actions of a few?"

"We expect you will honor the extraditions we have in progress, Mister Rojo."

"I am making no further commitments at this time."

"You aren't considering letting those men loose?"

"I am making no further commitments at this time, Mister Carter. My diplomatic staff will be in touch with your State Department in a few days, and we will schedule meetings to discuss this further."

Carter fell silent a moment. Rojo glanced at Esteves with a hopeful look.

"We will expect to hear from them soon, Mister Rojo. Thank you for taking my call."

The American hung up. Rojo handed the receiver back to Esteves, who returned it to the hook.

"Well?" the younger man said.

Rojo only shook his head.

CHAPTER 27

The White House, Oval Office

PRESIDENT JACK CARTER put down the phone and looked at the faces of the other men in the Oval Office who had listened on extensions.

One of the three men stood and began pacing. He was Attorney General Mike Turner, and President Carter didn't tell him to sit. Turner, more than anybody in the room, had a reason to feel disturbed by Rojo's statements.

"That was—" the president began.

"Unreal, sir," said the director of the Drug Enforcement Administration. He sat on a couch across from the president's desk, along with the Attorney General, and the man in charge of the Central Intelligence Agency's Anti-Drug section.

"Unreal is a very good word for it."

Turner removed his wire-framed glasses and aimed the glasses at every man in the room. "It's *disgusting. Outrageous.* What the hell is that man *thinking?*"

President Jack Carter watched Turner with sympathy. The man had lost his daughter to cocaine addiction. As Carter's Attorney General, he'd made the drug war top priority, often coordinating with Team Reaper in their operations.

"What are we going to do, Jack?" Turner said.

Carter paused to consider his answer. "Rojo campaigned on ending the drug war, but he never gave any indication that total surrender was what he meant."

"We assumed," the DEA chief said, "that he meant an increase in military operations."

Turner snapped to the CIA man, Don Hensley. "Did your people know anything about this, Don?"

"Nothing."

"Your people heard *nothing* about a total surrender?"

Hensley remained steady under the fiery gaze of the Attorney General. "Mike, if nobody's talking, my people aren't hearing anything. And I assure you, *nobody* in Mexico City was talking about this."

"What about informants in the cartels? Surely they were approached about this?"

Hensley shook his head.

"*Outrageous!*" Turner repeated. He jammed his glasses back on and resumed pacing around the office. "We've spent tens of millions of dollars to fight this problem. I can't believe he wants to flush all that hard work away."

The CIA man said to Carter, "I do have one suggestion, Mister President."

"Let's hear it."

"I had our financial people dig into Rojo's various

accounts," Hensley said, "and like his predecessors, he's receiving cash payments from shell companies we've identified as being connected with various cartels. They chip in money that goes to various national leaders and law enforcement personnel, and the shell companies are the pots the money is distributed from."

"Have the payments stopped?" the president asked.

"No, sir. His most recent payment was two days ago. It suggests the cartels have not taken him off the payroll, which means he's already completed his negotiations with them and there will be no interruption in whatever previous arrangements they've made with the government."

Turner snapped, "I'm not hearing any suggestions out of this, Don."

Carter said, "Mike? Sit down. Settle down. We aren't going to solve anything by blowing up at each other."

Mike Turner said, "My apologies, Mister President," and dropped unsteadily onto the couch beside the DEA director. He looked at the floor.

Hensley opened his mouth to continue, but the president raised a hand. The man closed his mouth. Carter said, "We don't need to debate whether or not Rojo has already met with the cartels. The meetings happened. It has always been frustrating to me that we're spending as much money as we are down there, and half the people we work with are on the take. Every now and then we take down a big shot, but there is always another to take his place."

"There is somebody in Rojo's inner circle, sir," Hensley continued, "who might be able to help us."

"How?"

"Rojo's wife. Perlita is her name. She lost her family to the cartels. You can bet she won't be any happier about this turn of events than we are."

"Can we use her to get to him?"

"I was thinking something more direct, sir. Use her to *expose* him. He's still on the take. If we can show the Mexican public that he's more concerned with keeping his pockets lined than being serious about ending the drug war, we might spark a popular uprising, a recall election, whatever you want to call it, and get somebody in that office who isn't an idiot."

The DEA man chuckled quietly.

"You mean discredit him," Carter said, "and maybe force a resignation?"

"Exactly."

"Does the Agency have assets already in place?"

"Of course, sir."

"I'm worried those assets might be compromised just like Team Reaper."

"They've reported no problems so far, sir."

"That doesn't mean they're home free. We need to have a conversation with the Mexican government on the details about the extraditions, and a few other questions I have. If that doesn't go well, we will proceed with your plan, Don. But if there's *any* hint that the cartels are coming after your agents, I want those people pulled out of there. It might be better to send Team Reaper back. They'll be spoiling for a fight anyway."

"OK, sir."

"That's all for now, gentleman. Thank you for coming. I wish we were ending on a higher note."

Carter watched the three men leave. They left him in the office. Alone. The burden of leadership was a tough one, and Carter's shoulders felt heavy. But they'd survive this crisis like they had many others. He would not let present circumstances wear him down.

There were too many people counting on him.

CHAPTER 28

Lafayette Square, Washington, D.C.

DIEGO MEDINA STOOD in the shadow of the Rochambeau Statue in the southwest corner of Lafayette Square, keeping an eye on the exit of the West Wing across Pennsylvania Ave. Three cars sat under the overhang, and presently three men exited the building. Medina did not make out their faces, but he had a very good idea he was looking at Attorney General Mike Turner, CIA anti-drug station chief Don Hensley, and DEA Director William Warner. He'd have loved to be a fly on the wall in the Oval Office during their meeting with President Jack Carter.

The big black cars left the West Wing, turned onto Pennsylvania, and departed. Medina quickly lost sight of the cars, but it was no matter.

He looked up at Rochambeau, the statue honoring a French nobleman who helped the American colonies win their Revolution. He spit on the base of the statue. If the French had stayed home, maybe American wouldn't be such a problem for Medina and his employers.

He left the statue, walking up Jackson Place to H St, where he turned right. A block away was his next destination, a sandwich shop, where he knew his next contact was already waiting.

He found Boris Yakovlev sitting in a back corner with a corned beef on rye.

Medina dropped into the chair opposite the big man.

"You didn't wait?"

Yakovlev shrugged. "They serve quickly. You won't be waiting long."

Medina shook his head and left the table, ordering at the counter, returning with his own sandwich and drink. He noted the Russian's black coffee. He wondered if the big man spiked it with vodka. Medina had known many Russian operatives and mercenaries over the years; they always seemed to carry a flask of vodka in their back pockets.

Medina bit into his turkey and bacon sandwich. "What is the latest?" he said.

"Mendez failed in Mexico," Yakovlev said.

"Reaper is still alive?"

"All of them."

"And Mendez?"

"Dead. Blew up in his helicopter."

Medina shook his head and ate some more.

The Russian said, "Team Reaper will remain a thorn in our side. They will jeopardize the rest of the mission."

"Where are they now?"

"I don't know, but they aren't here. That's for sure.

Our spies in El Paso report they haven't returned to any of their homes, either."

"That means they're running," Medina said. "That means we're basically free and clear. They'll spend days trying to figure out their next move now that they have no infrastructure, and within that time, we'll have made our moves. We will be long gone before they get to D.C."

Yakovlev sipped some coffee. "You're more optimistic than I."

Medina shrugged. "We have a job to do. I'm not going to dwell on difficulties we haven't faced yet."

"Speaking of which?"

Medina put down his sandwich, still chewing a bite, and dug a thumb drive out of the inside pocket of his jacket. He passed the thumb drive to the Russian and swallowed. "Everything you need is there."

Yakovlev took the thumb drive and dropped it into his shirt pocket.

"Time table also included, so our strikes are coordinated," Medina said. "I don't see a need for us to meet again."

"Fair enough," Yakovlev said. He swallowed some more coffee.

New Mexico, Outside Alamogordo

It was dark, cold, and uncomfortable, but Roger Cross of the New Mexico Citizens Militia was having the time of his life.

The rest of his five-man team weren't complaining, either.

Sheriff Vic Nazarian had sealed the deal with the militia after informing them that help would also come from a secret strike team the government was sending, an off-the-books effort from a general Nazarian had once served with in the Rangers.

Nazarian's speech to the militia group had certainly produced its share of hoots and questions from the rank and file, but the group voted to go with the plan because they saw the damage caused by an open border, and the Feds not giving a crap what happened to them.

Having the strike force available to take the heat off meant they could also act as shadow fighters in the battle.

Cross had been disappointed with those voting against the effort, but he knew deep down that some members weren't in it for the fight. They were indeed overgrown Boy Scouts, helpful in times of disaster, but skittish when the time came to actually take up arms and defend their country.

"I think I see something," Cross said into his Motorola com unit.

Cross and his team were decked out in dark fatigues, full weapons and web gear, ready to strike. They waited atop a rise overlooking one of the roads leading from the border. Two other teams had other roads similarly staked out. They were looking for drug traffic, and, to Cross, the truck he spotted through his high-powered binoculars looked like a prime target.

"Confirmed," said teammate Billy Trache. He was watching the road from a position below the ridge.

"Two men, pick-up truck, the bed is covered. Mexico plates."

"It matches the profile Nazarian told us about," Cross said, "but we can't open fire until we're sure."

"Roadblock standing by."

The roadblock, featuring the three remaining members of Cross's team, was a staged accident, complete with flares. The incoming truck would certainly see the glowing torches in the darkness surrounding the area well outside the city.

They needed the truck to stop.

And then they needed the two occupants to give them a reason to shoot.

CHAPTER 29

CROSS REACHED a nook near the side of the road as the truck in question neared the "accident" scene with the three militiamen at the cars waving the truck to a stop. The three men wore long coats to conceal their weapons and webbing. Cross, with Trache also nearby, lined up the suspects in the sights of their semi-automatic rifles. Each carried a custom-built variant of the AR-15.

Cross sighted on the passenger, who fidgeted as the driver tried to not answer any questions about help and instead demanded passage.

The passenger eventually noticed one of Cross' people slipping around the back of the truck. He shouted an alarm. The driver reached for something under the dash and stuck a gun out the window.

Two pops and the driver's head snapped back; the shots fired by Trache from his position. Cross snapped back the trigger on his rifle, but the .223 slug deflected as it punched through the windshield. The passenger dived out of the way, his door opening, the pudgy man jumping out with a machine pistol in his right hand.

Cross shouted for his guys to get down, firing, Trache firing as well, the slugs jolting the pudgy man as he stood in the road.

The drug thug fell forward and hit the tarmac hard.

"Anybody hurt?" Cross shouted, breaking cover to approach the phony accident scene. His men reported no injuries other than scrapes as they hit the deck.

Trache joined the group, scanning for more threats, his AR tucked tightly into his shoulder.

"Get the gas," Cross said, "and let's move this truck off the roadway. I want it lit up for the pictures we're going to spread around the city."

The idea had actually come from the mind of Bill Trache. Cross had insisted nothing be posted on social media about their activities, by flyers around town could give warning to any drug thugs who saw them that their contraband was not getting past the city border.

Cross hoped it put a scare into them, but he also knew, next time, they'd come with more shooters.

———

Alamogordo, White Sands Regional Airport

Sheriff Vartan "Vic" Nazarian and Deputy Keely Lynton waited by a private hangar on the south end of the airport, in the middle of nowhere, the airport nestled in a notch between the 54 and 70 freeways.

Nazarian knew a bunch of Washington spooks were involved because the hangar, vacant for months, suddenly had a buyer, and General Jones, in a follow-up call, had directed Nazarian to meet a private jet at that hangar. He assured the sheriff that John Kane and his Team Reaper would be aboard.

Nazarian didn't keep secrets from Keely Lynton. She'd been his right-hand for many years. She was also a by-the-book cop, but she had a similar feeling to his regarding drug-related violence, and had warmed to his idea of using the militia far better than he thought she would.

He was happy with their score the night before. They both were. Cross has reported early in the morning. The best part was that none of Cross's people had been hurt.

That wouldn't always be the case, though. He hoped the militiamen understood what they were facing.

A light wind blew across the airfield but did nothing to cool the heat from the overhead sun. Deputy Lynton, with her ball cap and sunglasses, didn't complain. She looked out on the desolation around them.

"You sure about these people?" she said, finally breaking the silence, asking a question Nazarian had expected, but he hadn't expected her to wait so long to ask.

"I'm sure about very little right now, Keely. All I know is we need help, and General Jones said this crew can help us."

"They're not cops."

"No, they aren't."

"The last thing we need is the military here, Sheriff."

"Do me a favor, and give them a chance."

She didn't say "yay" or "nay". Nazarian decided to take it as a "maybe".

———

John Kane looked out the window at the brown landscape below.

The CIA's Citation Mustang was well-equipped. Leather seats, plenty to eat and drink, video entertainment options, the whole nine. But the team wasn't having it. They were exhausted, spread out through the cabin, trying to rest. If they were anything like Kane, rest eluded them. Because the flight took Team Reaper over El Paso before entering New Mexico, and all they could think about was their Team Bravo colleagues probably dying in a hospital and General Jones not telling them the whole story.

Kane had only one other thought besides the survival of his friends.

Revenge.

Whoever was responsible, whoever had also tried to kill Kane and his crew in Mexico, was going to dearly pay for what they had done.

Yet, somehow, the pledge of vengeance didn't calm Kane's mind at all.

The jet began its descent, the pilot advising so over the intercom, Kane suggesting that everybody get their gear together so they were ready to step off the plane as soon as they reached the hangar. Everybody gave him the stink eye. Of course they had to do that. He was being bossy for the sake of being bossy, to keep his mind off what everybody else was thinking, and they were irritable for the same reason.

The Citation's wheels chirped as the plane touched down, and it was a short ride to the hangar on the south end. Kane saw the two cops waiting for them, and the two Sheriff's Department SUVs he assumed was their transportation into the city.

"Look at all the desert," Brick said, peering out a side window.

Axe said, "Is this New Mexico or Afghanistan?"

"Flip a coin," Brick said.

"I want tacos," Cara, not looking out a window, proclaimed.

"We'll get squared away and then go looking for tacos," Kane said.

Only Carlos Arenas said nothing as the plane finally came to a stop. Kane watched the former member of the Mexican Special Forces. He had a thousand-yard stare on his face. His mind was elsewhere, and not only with Team Bravo. Arenas was the only member of the team with a family, and if the enemy had hit Bravo, his kids might be on the target list too.

General Jones needed to come across with more information to set the team at ease or this fight would be their biggest challenge yet.

CHAPTER 30

NAZARIAN AND LYNTON introduced themselves as Team Reaper stepped off the jet, and helped the team load their gear into the back of the SUVs. Kane drove with Nazarian, Cara and Axe in the back seat. Deputy Lynton drove with Brick and Arenas. There was no way Kane was going to let Axe Burton have any chance to pull his Romeo act on Deputy Lynton.

Kane knew nothing about Vartan "Vic" Nazarian except his name and that General Jones had served with him in the Rangers. He looked capable enough, certainly not weak, and wore his uniform with authority. But something on his face suggested nervous tension. He either wasn't sure he could trust Team Reaper, or he was about to drop a hot potato on them that not even General Jones had known about.

"What's the situation, Sheriff?" Kane finally said, to break the silence lingering in the vehicle.

"I'd prefer to answer that when we get to the station," Nazarian replied, "when your team is together, and Deputy Lynton is present as well."

Hot potato, Kane thought.

Presently Nazarian turned into the parking lot of the Otero County Sheriff's Office. Team Reaper left their gear in the SUVs. When the team finally entered Nazarian's office, he dismissed Deputy Lynton, shut the door, and told the team to find a seat wherever.

Kane and Cara dropped into the two seats in front of Nazarian's desk, while Brick, Axe, and Arenas sat around the room.

Kane crossed his legs. "Why do I get the feeling we're about to be dropped into a boiling pot of water?"

"Because you are," Nazarian said, handing Kane a sheet of paper with a picture and some words on it.

Cara leaned over to see the page. It showed a burning truck with the words, two bodies in the roadway, and masked gunmen. The words THIS IS WHAT HAPPENS TO DRUG THUGS WHO SNEAK OVER THE BORDER were under the picture.

"So?" Kane handed the picture to Arenas, who then passed it to Brick and Axe. "Looks like somebody is doing your job, Sheriff. Is that the issue?"

"They're doing what I told them to do."

"Pardon?"

"I don't know what General Jones told you, Mister Kane, but the situation is serious enough that I asked for the help of the state citizens militia."

"Oh, no," Cara said.

"Oh, *yes*," Nazarian said. "They aren't bad people. They want to do something. And if the government won't, they're capable of doing it."

Nazarian spent the next ten minutes reviewing the recent murders, gap at the border, and his meetings with Roger Cross and the militiamen.

"This could get out of control really fast, Sheriff," Kane said. "Let us take over."

Nazarian shook his head. "They'll do what they do, you'll do what you do. What are your orders?"

"Get a briefing from you, and take care of the problem," Kane said. "You don't need a bunch of engineers and pharmacists getting involved."

"Civilians do not belong in this fight."

"Considering civilians are the ones who are dying, I disagree," Nazarian said. He didn't break eye-contact with Kane. He wasn't backing down.

Kane knew a fighter when he saw one, and Nazarian was not going to go away quietly. It might be better, he decided, to see how this plays out.

"It's your county, Sheriff," Kane said. "We're here to help. This is what we do. It's going to get bloody, and none of the blood will be on your hands."

"Good."

"Unless—"

Nazarian cut off the objection with a wave. "It's settled, Mister Kane. The militia have their plans. In fact, without them, you don't have a safehouse."

"Fair enough."

"If your team would like to get settled at the hotel, we can meet for dinner and go over a few more things."

"That would be ideal," Kane said.

Nazarian rose from his seat. "Let's go then."

Kane followed Nazarian out of the office, not noticing the curious looks that passed between the rest of his teammates.

This wasn't going to be another routine mission.

Kane unpacked what little street clothing items he had and made a note to make a run to Target or find a mall so he could buy some more things. He'd tell the rest of the crew the same, even though they were probably thinking the same thing as he.

He stashed the case containing his weapons and web gear in the closet. As he slid the door shut, somebody knocked on the door.

Through the peephole, Cara stood on the other side. Kane let her in and shut the door.

"What are you thinking?" he said.

She stood in the room with folded arms. "This is nuts."

"I agree."

"Are you going to tell General Jones?"

"I'm not telling Jones shit until I hear something more about Bravo."

He moved past her to the table up against the wall and sat down and brooded. Cara sat on the edge of the bed.

"After tonight," Kane said, "we'll have a better idea of how things stand around here, and then we can focus on getting even."

"Do you think these militia guys will be hard to handle?"

"They won't trust us, which bothers me, because if we're going to rely on them, we need to be one unit."

"I'm sure you can charm them."

There was no humor in the glare he gave her.

"Just kidding, Reaper; calm down."

He sighed. His expression softened. "You ever just want to go home and hide?" he said.

"All the time," she told him.

CHAPTER 31

West Coast of Mexico, Estate of Chucho Banderas

THE TABLE HAD a spread of food that Chucho Banderas figured would be enough for his guest, and so far, they'd made only a very small dent in the number of items offered.

Victor Zamorano sat back in his chair and let out a satisfied burp. He laughed. "My apologies, Chucho."

The cartel leader laughed. "None necessary. My chef is one of the best in the world."

Waiters hovered, refreshing drinks and fetching anything either cartel boss needed. They sat on the outdoor patio of Chucho's mansion overlooking the Pacific, the raging ocean far enough away to transfix anyone gazing upon its vastness.

"I suppose we should talk business now," Zamorano said.

Chucho Banderas wiped his mouth with a napkin. "Yes. We must talk business. Much is taking place."

Armed guards floated at the far end of the balcony, out of earshot, out of mind. More prowled the grounds below the balcony. Chucho Banderas lived like a man with no cares in the world, and his extravagance within the house spoke to that lifestyle. He spared no expense; only the best.

"Let's review," Banderas said. "We've received enough tips from our friends in the government to interrupt anti-drug operations and disable entire police units who aren't listening to the president's stand-down orders."

Zamorano nodded.

"Military units are returning to their bases and abandoning previous operations."

Zamorano nodded again.

"Team Reaper survived."

Zamorano cursed. He said, "We succeeded in El Paso."

"No deaths have been confirmed from our strike there."

"Only because we can't get anybody into the hospital to check. Which means there are people worth protecting."

"They're crippled. Team Reaper is without resources of any kind."

"I'm not sure that matters," Zamorano said. "They've never been handicapped by such difficulties before."

"They've never been *hurt* like this before."

"Do we know where they are now?"

"We are positive they are no longer in Mexico."

"That doesn't reassure me," Zamorano said. "Is there a way to find them?"

"Where could they have gone? Say they are somewhere in the US. They can't return to El Paso; their
headquarters is wiped out. They're on the run. Maybe
that's exactly where we want them."

"On the run and ineffective?"

"Precisely," Banderas said.

Zamorano paused in thought, and Chucho
Banderas wondered if his associate in the conspiracy
would be satisfied. If Team Reaper turned up, they
could deal with them. If the team remained hidden,
underground, stashed away at a safe house, and couldn't
bother them or make their way to Mexico, what did it
hurt? The goal had been to kill them, yes. But having
them out of commission wasn't a bad result either.

A guard carrying an automatic rifle across his back
emerged from the house, approaching Banderas and
handed him a phone.

"Medina, sir."

Chucho Banderas took the phone. Zamorano
stopped thinking whatever he was thinking and
watched Banderas take the call.

"Yes, Diego," Banderas said.

"We're ready. Targets located. Do we have your
authorization to engage?"

Banderas smiled. When he'd told *El Cortador* to
check in before acting on his mission orders, the
assassin had not been pleased. He did not understand
the delicacy of the mission. Should the slightest error or
delay occur, the Cutter could not proceed. Thankfully,
the problems Banderas had been concerned about had
not happened, so the killer was free and clear to carry
out his mission.

Banderas told him so.

"Keep an eye on the news," *el Cortador* said.

"One more thing," Banderas said, thinking of how he could please Zamorano regarding Team Reaper. "We will need you and the others to remain in the US. Team Reaper may be licking wounds somewhere, and when they show their faces, we'll want them blown away."

"I'll take care of Team Reaper *gratis*, Mister Banderas."

"Are you speaking for your Russian friend as well?" Banderas chuckled.

"He'll want more money."

"He'll have it. As will you, *el Cortador*. I don't expect anybody to work for free."

"Anything else?" the assassin said.

"Good luck, Diego."

Medina hung up without saying goodbye. Banderas handed the phone back to the guard, who took it and returned to the interior of the house.

Banderas raised an eyebrow at his guest. "Well?"

"Keeping the team there, on stand-by, will help," Zamorano said. "Reaper will eventually pull itself together and become a nuisance once again. They *must* be stamped out completely."

"They have meddled in our business for the last time indeed, Victor."

Zamorano smiled.

The White House, Oval Office

The call was not going well.

Not at all.

Secretary of State Frank Muir spoke on the line with Rojo's representative, Federico Esteves, in the Oval Office. He sat in front of the president's desk, the phone on his side of the desk, the speaker on so all could hear.

Muir was joined by Attorney General Mike Turner, who sat to his left.

Carter sat back in his chair, keeping still. He didn't want the Mexican representative to know he was listening.

"Mister Esteves," Muir said, his voice sounding perpetually tired. "I cannot believe what you have just said."

"Do you need me to repeat it, Mister Secretary?"

Carter, Muir and Turner exchanged shocked looks.

Carter shook his head. The petulance of the New Mexican administration dumbfounded him. What were they thinking?

Of their own pocketbooks.

Muir continued. "We have a deal with your government, Mister Esteves. Going back on extradition agreements is not something we will tolerate."

"We are not unreasonable," Estevez said. "We will extradite the top two kingpins on the list, and the rest will remain in Mexico. We will try them here."

"Or?"

"Or nothing, Mister Secretary. That is none of your business. Mexico is asserting its rights in this manner. We are not subservient to the United States."

Muir glanced at Carter. The president nodded. Muir said, "But you like our money, right?"

"Pardon?"

"We understand your nation is under new leadership with its own agenda," Muir said. "The same thing happens in the United States at least every eight years. The changes to agreements we have already made is, as I said, not acceptable. Tell President Rojo that unless all extraditions are honored, Mexico will face sanctions. We will seal the border with federal troops and current deportations will be expedited and anybody from your country trying to illegally cross our border will face prosecution."

Silence on the other end of the line.

"Did you hear me, Mister Esteves?"

"Loud and clear, Mister Secretary. We will be in touch."

The line clicked.

President Carter leaned forward and turned off the speakerphone. He rested his arms on his desktop.

"Well, gentlemen?"

Mike Turner said, "This is a load of crap."

"That very well may be," the president said, "but it's where we're at. We have only one option. We proceed with Don Hensley's plan to try and get Rojo's wife on our side, and initiate a campaign to force the man's resignation."

Neither Muir nor Turner argued.

CHAPTER 32

McLean, VA, CIA Headquarters

DON HENSLEY, alone in his office, put down the phone and sighed. All right, then. If POTUS wanted to proceed with his earlier suggestion, he'd get the ball rolling straight away.

He picked up the phone again and dialed another number. The other party picked up after three rings.

"Yes?"

"It's Don at HQ."

"What's going on?"

"We have something cooking in Mexico and I need you and your team to get down there. Can you meet me at the usual place and we'll talk it over?"

"I need a half hour."

"See you then."

Hensley hung up. It would take him that long to get to the meet anyway, so he rose from his desk, grabbed his coat from the rack behind the door, and departed.

His car was later found halfway to his destination

riddled with machinegun fire and Hensley dead in the driver's seat.

———

DEA Director William Warner watched the garage door close behind him before stepping into his home. His wife was out for the night, helping her church group cook food for an upcoming event on Sunday. He left his keys on a wall hook in the kitchen and started down the hall to change out of his suit.

Two hours later, when his wife came home, she found him dead on their bedroom floor, bleeding from a slashed throat.

———

El Cortador waited till dark to make his move on Attorney General Mike Turner.

This was *his* kill.

The home in Capitol Heights, Maryland, off Riba Court and Brooke Road sat alone in a lot populated mostly by trees on either side of Riba, with a smattering of other homes and buildings in the otherwise secluded area.

The only fly in the ointment of hitting the AG Turner at his home was the black SUV that waited outside his residence, the engine running, when he was home, in case he needed to be quickly spirited to the White House in an emergency.

The SUV wasn't there now. Which meant Mike Turner was not home. Which meant Medina had time to set an ambush.

He swept the forest area with a casual walk through the lot, noting no security traps. He knew the SUV which transported Mike Turner wasn't armored and he only had two marshals guarding him. He did not get the full security and armored vehicle treatment the Secretary of State received.

Decked out in black, his getaway vehicle nearby, armament ready, Diego Medina waited in the forest for the SUV to appear. It had to turn from Brooke Road onto Riga, and when it slowed at the corner for the right-hand turn, Medina planned to strike.

He saw the headlights first.

He clicked off the safety on the HK M320 grenade launcher. In the breech waited a high-explosive cartridge he planned to shoot into the front grill. His submachine gun would take care of the rest.

The black SUV slowed for the turn onto Riga Court and Medina fired the grenade launcher. At a distance of about 15 yards, the projectile reached the front grill in a flash, the blast exploding the front end of the car. The hood swung up, crashing into the windshield, as the vehicle swerved off the road into the right-side tree line where it stopped short of plowing into the trees when the front wheels hit a ditch.

Shouts from the vehicle as the two marshals in front piled out, guns up. One ran to a back door.

Medina raised the SMG and let a burst go. A flash hider would have been nice, but he wasn't worried about the flame from the muzzle marking his position. The marshal on the driver's side let out a yell as he fell against the body of the car, his useless handgun falling from his grasp.

The other marshal opened fire over the hood, single

shots peppering the forest around him, but none coming close. Medina fired another burst that missed. The small part of the marshal he'd been aiming for was too small after all.

Medina slapped a fresh magazine into the SMG and left his position, zigzagging through the trees as the marshal fired blindly. The Cutter kept his weapon close to his chest, getting closer to the road. The marshal kept scanning for a target while shouting into his radio. No sign of Attorney General Mike Turner, but Medina knew he was there, hiding behind his bodyguard.

Medina stopped short of the road and used a tree as a brace as he lined up the marshal in his sights.

CHAPTER 33

MIKE TURNER, on his hands and knees, stayed by the passenger side rear tire as the marshal tried to take out the attacker and call for back-up at the same time. He wanted to run around the other side of the vehicle and grab the other gun, but that would put him in plain view, make him an easy target, and he didn't want the cartel to get him that easily.

Then the marshal's voice was cut mid-sentence by a burst of submachine gun fire that took off the top of his head. Turner shut his eyes as the man's body fell beside him, scrambling underneath the SUV, his coat catching, tearing, on something, the heat from the underside scorching. He stayed put, his eye on the gap surrounding the vehicle.

He watched a portion of the killer's legs and boots gain the roadway and stalk toward the SUV.

Taking a deep breath, Mike Turner shuffled on his stomach to the opposite side of the SUV, clearing the vehicle and making a mad grab for the first marshal's fallen pistol.

His move surprised the assassin, who stopped in the center of the road, as if frozen. Turner took the advantage. He wrapped his hands around the grips of the automatic and lifted the pistol. That's when his surprise move ran out of dividends. The assassin let off another squirt from the short-barreled submachine gun, and Turner felt a rip in the center of his belly spill his guts onto the pavement and another rip through his upper chest. He fell hard on his back, eyes staring skyward, thoughts of his late wife and daughter passing through his mind as his vision faded.

Otero County, New Mexico

The safe house sat in the hills outside of Alamogordo and Team Reaper were glad to see it was fully equipped with food and other required items.

There wasn't time to take in the luxuries or explore the area around the cabin, but the small hills and wooded landscape made for defensible positions should they be required. Kane would scout the area later. For now, there was work to be done. Kane and his crew were briefly introduced to Roger Cross and his militiamen, and then General Jones called to tell him to get on Skype because the pizza was hitting the fan in D.C. and plans were changing.

A large dinner table in the living room housed Team Reaper and the others as General Jones addressed the group over Skype. The laptop with his face on the monitor sat in the center of the table.

"It's getting bad here," the general said. "We've had

three assassinations in the last several hours. Director of the DEA, CIA's anti-drug section chief, and Attorney General Mike Turner."

"How is this connecting with Rojo in Mexico?" Kane said. He sat closest to the computer.

"We're not sure," the general said. "But we know there's a connection, somehow. It might be part of the deal he made with the cartels that included turning you over to them. We simply don't know. But President Carter has an idea on how we can find out."

"We're listening," Kane said. He looked around the table at the rest of his team, all of whom paid careful attention to the general's words.

"Don Hensley came up with the idea before he was killed. We need somebody back in Mexico to make contact with Rojo's wife. Her family was killed by a cartel, they wanted her family farm, and we think we can turn her to our side. Find proof of Rojo's deal with the cartels, and expose them. Force his resignation."

"We know plenty of people who could help with that, sir," Kane said.

"Assuming they aren't dead. We don't know how far this killing machine reaches."

Kane turned to Carlos and Brick. "You two can head back. Carlos, surely your old comrades in the special forces can help."

"Probably," Arenas said. "Want me to make some calls?"

Kane nodded. Arenas left the table.

Kane turned back to the laptop screen. "What if she won't cooperate, General?"

"We still need to find the truth about Rojo's

arrangement. Find somebody who knows, and work 'em over."

"Yes, sir."

"Everything satisfactory so far?"

"Cabin's nice, Nazarian is great, the associates he has seem okay." Kane didn't look around the room for a reaction. He wasn't sure about the militiamen. They seemed capable, they had perfectly good bona fides as far as combat experience went, but he distrusted vigilantes. He didn't know if they had their own agenda, or would respond to his instructions.

Only one way to find out.

"I'll keep you updated," the general said.

"Sir?"

"Yes?"

"Update on El Paso?"

The general paused a moment. Cara got Kane's attention and mouthed "Thank you" at him.

"Everybody remains stable," the general said. "Stable is improving I believe were Doctor Morales' words."

"Very good, sir, thank you."

The Skype session ended. Kane closed the laptop.

"When I worked for Jones," Nazarian said, "he was more of a ball-buster."

Kane turned. The sheriff sat on the back of a nearby couch, leaning over slightly with his hands resting above his knees.

"He can be," Kane said. "Right now, I think we're a little preoccupied."

Deputy Lynton, near Nazarian said, "Time to tell them?"

"Tell us what?" Kane said.

Nazarian said, "If you're sending two of your men back across the border, I think I know something the rest of you can do."

Axe jumped in. "What's that?"

Lynton rolled her eyes at the ex-Recon Marine sniper. Axe Burton had already tried to charm the female deputy, and she'd rebuffed him smartly.

"A processing plant," Nazarian said. "Outside the county."

"Is that where all the shipments have been going to?"

"In the trucks, yeah. They bring the raw stuff over the border and refine it at the processing plant. Somehow it's better than finalizing the product on the Mexico side."

"Uh-huh," Cara said. "But you said outside the county."

"It's out of our jurisdiction," Lynton said. "Technically, it's in Federal territory."

"Even if we could raid the place," Nazarian said, "I don't have the people to deal with the military firepower we'd be facing."

Kane added, "But maybe we can knock it out. Got any pictures?"

"I have a map," Nazarian said. He slid off the couch to get his briefcase out of the SUV.

CHAPTER 34

"I'D RATHER GO to Washington, Reaper," said Axe.

Cara agreed.

"Our best bet," Kane said, "is to stay here. Cause enough trouble that the cartel has to come to us. Then we can break some legs and find out what's happening on this side of the border."

"What if Arenas and Brick fail?" Cara said.

Brick jumped in. "Dammit, Cara—"

"Seriously. Getting the wife to turn? That's a tall order."

"We'll figure it out, Cara," Kane said. "We always do." He turned to Roger Cross. His militiamen sat behind him on the floor, all of them focused on the team at the table.

"Cross, we're going to need ammo. Nine-millimeter and two-two-three. Can you help?"

Cross laughed. "Hell, we got ammo coming out our ears, Reaper. Most of us are preppers, remember?"

Kane smiled. "Consider this our doomsday

scenario. We need whatever you can provide. I promise you'll receive replacements in return once this is over."

"If we all live," one of the militiamen called out.

"I'm not dying in New Mexico," Kane said. "It's nice here, but this won't be my last stop. When I'm dying, I'll be on a beach."

The militiamen only nodded.

"That's the attitude you have to have," Kane said. "We might not be invincible in reality, but we have to think we are. Negative thoughts will get you killed."

The front door opened and slammed as Nazarian returned with his briefcase. Team Reaper made room for him at the table. From the briefcase he pulled out a map of the county, spreading the paper out, everybody gathering around as he pointed to the processing plant location with a finger. Kane handed him a pen. Nazarian made a circle.

"It's there," the sheriff said.

Nazarian looked unsure of himself. Kane studied the sheriff's face. He didn't know if Nazarian was unsure of his claim, or if he was getting nervous about the overall operation. Or maybe the strain of keeping everything together was getting to him.

I certainly know a thing or two about that...

"We'll go," Kane told him. "Your people stay here. That includes you, Cross."

"Okay," Cross said. "We'll keep up our regular patrol."

"Good idea," Kane said. "Sheriff, is there anything else?"

Nazarian shook his head. "Not from me. Is it a good time to get the grill going?"

"We got beer?" Kane said.

"There's beer."

"Then I think it's a great time," Kane said.

Axe added, "My stomach's been grumbling since we started!"

Keely Lynton rolled her eyes again.

———

Dinner consisted of Caesar salad, steaks, corn on the cob, and plenty of beer. Cross and the militiamen handled the cooking chores, and they served food cooked to perfection. When the beer started flowing, Roger Cross told his men not to get too sloshed. Kane seconded the order to his own people.

Axe said, "Party pooper."

Kane grinned at Axe. He'd tried to sit next to Keely Lynton after she found a place to eat, but she'd immediately left the spot to find another. Axe looked quite frustrated. He'd finally found the one woman on the planet seemingly immune to his alleged charm.

After dinner, once the sun had gone down, Kane found Nazarian out front staring into the distance. Crickets chirped. The night chill was quite comfortable after the warmth of the cabin. Kane stepped up beside the sheriff and handed him a bottle of water.

"Figure you're driving home soon."

Nazarian twisted off the cap. "Good thinking."

Kane drank some beer. "What's on your mind?"

"What do you mean?"

"You had a look back there I noticed. Either you aren't sure of the exact location of the processing plant, or you're unsure of this whole operation."

"I hate that it's come to this."

"I understand."

"Do you? You understand we seem to be living under a government that doesn't care about what happens outside D.C.?"

"It sure seems that way sometimes."

"The fact that your unit even exists—"

"You don't have to tell me, Sheriff."

Nazarian swallowed some water. "I know a thing or two about genocide, and the drug problem is causing a slow one. Nobody seems to get that."

"I get it," Kane said.

"We need *everybody* to get it."

"We'll reach that point. Someday."

"That's not soon enough."

"I'm not sure what else to tell you, Sheriff," Kane said. "I've been fighting this war a long time. It never stops. I used to think like you. It's pointless, we never win, the Feds won't let us win, all that. After some time alone, I've come to realize I have to wait for the rest of the world to catch up and catch on with what we're doing."

"They're late."

"They always are. Eventually they arrive."

"Some people think this poison should be legal."

"And when that happens, we'll find another war to fight. There will always be a war somewhere."

Nazarian said nothing more. Neither did Kane. They watched the horizon. Crickets chirped.

CHAPTER 35

The White House, Oval Office

PRESIDENT CARTER FACED the three men across from him and thought about his wife's words of advice that morning: *"You've survived worse, Jack. Don't give up."*

He didn't have the heart to point out that every crisis was worse than the last one, and the lessons learned from previous problems didn't usually work with the new one. They were facing a blank canvas, needing to create a solution to the problem.

Though she was right about the, *don't give up* part.

And starting with the three men in the Oval Office with him, President Carter planned to not only not give up, but give the enemy ten times what they'd dished out.

"I'm sorry we're meeting under these conditions," the president said.

The three men nodded. They were:

Deputy Attorney General Grant Stockwell.

Deputy DEA Director Alan Brinkley

Deputy CIA Anti-Drug Section Director Steve Ransom.

The "seconds" of the men killed, thrown into leadership positions after the triple tragedies that Washington authorities were still trying to sort out.

All they knew for sure was that three good men were dead.

"We need to catch these killers," the president said, "and find out who sent them, and how, if it does, the killings connect to Rojo in Mexico."

The CIA man, Steve Ransom, said, "You think this was government-sanctioned?"

"I think it's highly likely. Everything that's happened with Team Reaper suggests that Rojo is helping the cartels in exchange for agreeing to his peace plan."

Deputy Attorney General Grant Stockwell said, "Do we have some sort of plan to find out if that's true, Mister President?"

Carter breathed deep. The men before him were only the seconds-in-command of the men he normally dealt with. These men normally only heard about what he did from their now-deceased bosses. It meant they weren't read-in on the previous discussions Carter had with their predecessors.

He updated the trio on the plan of getting Rojo's wife to turn on him, since her family had been victims of previous cartel violence. Carter added that he had people carrying out the plan as they spoke.

Carter told them it was the only way to bring closure to the disaster. Get rid of Rojo. Close down whatever shenanigans he had going in Mexico City and get somebody in that office they could work with.

Mexico City, Presidential Palace

Perlita Terrazas-Rojo sat with her legs crossed, back straight, perfectly poised as every nation's first lady should be, or so she had been told. What she wanted to do was curl up in a corner and figure out how to set her husband straight on his foolish cartel arrangements. Actually, it was more than foolish. That wasn't a strong enough word. The associations he was forming were evil, beyond him, and he had to be stopped. Somehow.

At least it was warm out, typical for Mexico City, with blue sky above, though if she looked hard enough, Perlita Terrazas-Rojo could see a smokey haze in the distance.

She sat on the edge of the defunct water fountain in the center courtyard of the National Palace, staring into space, ignoring the wandering security guards who watched over her. Surrounding Mexico's first lady were the three levels of the palace, the interior rows of archways forming a square around her. Why archways? She always wondered what the designers had been thinking. And why so many? It was as if the architect had fallen in love with the archway and used the motif as much as possible. Then beyond the archways was the exterior walkway, and then doorways to interior portions of the palace.

All very neat and tidy but horribly repetitive, showing no imagination whatsoever.

But those thoughts were merely distractions to what was really occupying her mind.

Her husband was conspiring with killers. Men who shipped poison around the world, and suffered no punishment for doing so; in fact, the kingpins lived in luxury while causing an untold amount of suffering.

It had to stop. Somehow. She had to find a way.

Her assistant, Amaya Olmos, strode her way from a doorway to the left. She stopped a few feet away.

"Your husband has returned, ma'am."

Perlita looked up at Amaya, the woman a few years younger, but both similar in appearance that they'd been mistaken for sisters in the press.

"Where is he?"

"His office."

Perlita stood. She smoothed the front of her dress and said, "Wait in my suite, Amaya. I'm going to have words with my husband. There may be shouting."

"Yes, ma'am."

Perlita Terrazas-Rojo marched off to confront her husband.

CHAPTER 36

PRESIDENT LUCIO ROJO spoke into the telephone on his desk. He wasn't sitting; he stood behind the desk, as the call had come in as soon as he'd arrived. Federico Esteves stood nearby, watching him talk into the receiver.

"Are you sure about this?" the Mexican president said.

"We are positive," said the man on the other end. "The plan came from the horse's mouth. No question."

Rojo nodded. He wasn't looking at Esteves, though. His eyes were elsewhere, further away, staring into a future where interference from other nations such as the United States might be a thing of the past.

"The problem will be taken care of," Rojo said. He put the phone down on the cradle without saying goodbye.

He looked grimly at Esteves.

"The CIA is sending people here," he said, "to trap me. They want to turn Perlita against me."

"We had thought of the possibility."

"No, we discussed how to deal with her reaction, because of her family. We knew she might be a problem. We didn't expect the CIA would come and try and turn my wife against me."

Rojo, seething inside, kept his voice down. When he shouted, his voice carried throughout the palace, or at least seemed to. He didn't want any gossip about another tirade leaking to the press like the last one had a few months ago.

Then: "Lucio!"

Rojo turned to see his wife entering the office.

Before he responded, she snapped at Esteves. "Get out."

Esteves didn't move. He waited for Rojo to nod. Then he slipped past the first lady on his way out the door. She pushed the door shut.

Rojo turned on a heel and faced her with his hands behind his back.

"Is this the kind of welcome I get after being gone all day?"

"This is going too far, Lucio," she said, approaching him. He held up a hand to stop her. She stopped, but glared at him.

"This has nothing to do with you, my pearl."

"Do *not* call me that! How *dare* you!"

"We have to make sacrifices," Rojo said. "Our country is bleeding. The bleeding needs to stop."

"So you're making *deals* with these *madmen*?"

"I am doing what is right for our country."

She hissed through her nose.

"Perlita, I know. Believe me, I understand. I have not forgotten your own struggles and the damage done to your family. But can you see the greater good in this?"

"All I can see is my anger at what you're doing. It's wrong!"

He held up his hands in a silent plea. "Please. Perlita. Give me a chance. Give this plan a chance. When you see how our nation begins to prosper, I think you'll start to see things my way."

She scoffed. "All I hear from you is *me, me, I, my way, me, me* like you're an opera singer!"

Rojo took a deep breath. Her attitude was grating on his last inch of patience. She could be quiet and introspective at times, often seem like she was unwilling or unable to communicate what was on her mind; other times, such as now, she turned into an inferno all the water in the ocean couldn't extinguish.

"You are upset," Rojo told her. "You need to lay down and not come out until you have *calmed* down, my dear."

That's when she let off a string of curses, questioning his parentage, his sexuality, anything she could think of, in an expletive-laden flurry of words that ended with her slamming the door as she exited.

Rojo waited. The door opened again and Federico Esteves stepped into the office once again.

"Well?"

Rojo shook his head. What had been a good marriage was going to quickly erode. If the CIA reached her, she may very well indeed betray him.

"We may have to do something about her," he said.

Esteves didn't argue.

———

Perlita Terrazas-Rojo told Amaya Olmos, her assistant, to get out of her suite and promptly locked herself in the opulent room. She changed into more comfortable clothes and stretched out on her bed, staring at the ceiling. Her pulse pounded; her blood flowed heavily; she felt a flush of heat throughout her body.

Lucio had royally pissed her off.

She'd never forget the day her family was killed.

A cartel had wanted her family's farm on the coast, for poppy production. Her father had refused; the cartel had sent soldiers; her family had been slain. She only survived because she'd been in the city, in college. Having to drop out for half a year when the money ran out, she didn't re-enroll until she'd secured her own employment. Life had not been easy since, and the turbulence she'd become accustomed to showed no sign of settling.

Her husband might have meant well, but he had no idea how the cartel was going to throw this new arrangement back at him. They'd also blackmail him. Her husband would be forced to do whatever the cartel demanded. He'd be their puppet.

She had to figure out a solution.

Perhaps the Americans might be able to help. As she continued contemplating the ceiling, she started thinking about who she knew at the U.S. Embassy.

CHAPTER 37

Downtown Alamogordo

VINNY HAWKE FELT alive in the alley.

Not this alley in particular, but any alley. He liked blending with the shadows. He was short enough to be missed by passersby, blending with the shadows thanks to his dark clothes. He picked a new alley every night, hanging out where his customers could find him (and maybe the cops couldn't), passing along the product he kept close by (never keeping the shit on you was the first rule a pusher learned because if it was on you the cops could find it and that was a no-no if you wanted to build an empire) in exchange for cash.

He was in one of his alleys now, watching a busy street, sipping on hot green tea with a splash of lemon because Vinny Hawke like sophistication and sophisticated people drank green tea with lemon and if anybody said anything different, he'd blast them with his Smith & Wesson nine-mil. Nobody got between Vinny Hawke and his tea.

A motorcycle rumbled to the curb in front of the alley and made Vinny Hawke lower the steaming cup from his lips because day-um, gurrrrl, the hottie climbing off the bike was something else for sure. She pulled off the helmet to reveal a short haircut but Vinny Hawke didn't mind that. He liked everything else from the neck down, mostly.

When she approached, he started to chuckle. He hadn't seen her before. She was either a new customer or a cop or maybe a Fed.

"Vinny Hawke?" she said. She cocked her head to one side, one hand on her hip.

"That's me."

"I'm planning a party and I need a few things."

Vinny Hawke shrugged. "So?"

She cocked her head the other way. "The Mule told me to talk to you about what I need."

Vinny Hawke nodded. She could still be a cop, but that meant the Mule had been picked up, and the street would have been buzzing with the news had that happened. She wasn't a cop. She'd gone through the trouble to find him, and he owed her service. Vinny Hawke like to give good service to his customers because that way they'd keep coming back.

"All right, what do you want?"

She flicked her nose.

"I got it, sure. How much?"

"Party of one," she said. She smiled.

"You going to this party all by yourself?"

The smile lingered. "I thought you might be interested, too."

Vinny Hawke let out a low laugh. "Vinny don't get social with customers. But the offer is appreciated."

He looked her up and down. She looked very trim in the biker leather. When his eyes met her face again, her expression changed. So did Vinny Hawke's. He went from happy to grim because he saw the lady take a pistol out of the leather jacket and the suppressor attached at the end meant nobody would hear the crack of the gunfire over the traffic noise.

Nobody did.

———

Club Fireball, Alamogordo

Zane Dalton took the martini from the burly bartender and swallowed part of the elixir. He didn't leave any money. He never had to pay for drinks. He had an exclusive arrangement with the club owner. In exchange for helping keep the party going, he got free drinks.

He didn't deal in the hard stuff. No cocaine, heroin, nothing like that for him. He was the pill guy. Uppers, downers, oxy, Vicodin, all that jazz, he had to be careful how he moved otherwise the pill containers in his pockets rattled. He was a reject out of 90210 (the original series) and his boyish looks and perfect blond hair made him irresistible to the females and even some of the dudes whom he had to politely brush off if he wanted to keep their business.

Club Fireball had a huge dance floor, low lighting, and plenty of party-goers to keep Dalton's attention. He sold his pills and collected money and all went well for the evening. Another successful night. No stress. He barely had to leave the barstool to earn his minimum for the night.

At the end of the night he walked out to the parking lot where his BMW 7-Series sat, and drove away from the club. He usually waited for most of the clientele to depart, so it was 2:30 in the morning when he drove through the intersection heading across town to his duplex.

While waiting at a light, jamming to some old school Hendrix, another car pulled up beside him. Zane Dalton glanced at the car. It was a nice ride, two dudes in front, and the man in the passenger seat was looking at him. Zane Dalton didn't like the look. Dude had a square jaw, short-cropped black hair. He looked like one hundred other Hispanics in the city, so Zane had no idea who he was. He rolled down his window and motioned for Zane to do the same. Zane shook his head. He looked at the traffic light. It was still red.

Movement. Dalton snapped his attention to the Hispanic in the other car and his eyes widened and his foot moved to the accelerator. The dude was pointing a gun at him. Zane Dalton's foot started to press on the gas pedal, but then the pressure stopped because a bullet went through Dalton's window and into his face. His body jerked with the impact, straining against the seat belt. He slumped in the seat. His car started across the intersection, but since there was no other traffic, it simply drifted across to bump into a light pole and stop.

The other car made an illegal left turn and sped away.

———

On the northern end of the city, a two-story house on an anonymous corner exploded without warning, as if a gas line had ruptured, but the blast didn't affect any of the other homes in the neighborhood.

Police and emergency crews swarmed over the area as the house burned, and in case there was a gas leak, evacuated nearby homes, closing off streets, generally going by the book to protect the public from potential danger until they'd determined once and for all if there actually *was* danger.

By sunrise, a lot of information had been gathered about the house that went *ka-blooey* with three people and a crap ton of drugs inside.

One, they learned from detectives that it was a known drug supply house, and the residents sometimes sold narcotics at the front door.

Two, the three who died included a man named Blake Jarvis, who'd so far managed to avoid police custody by never being exactly where the cops needed him to be (i.e., near any evidence) so his death actually pleased the officers who had tried for so long to put cuffs on his wrists.

The third thing cops learned was that two other major drug pushers had been killed in other parts of the city.

They wondered who was doing the killing.

They didn't particularly want to find out, though. They had better things to do.

CHAPTER 38

Outside Otero County, The Desert

JOHN KANE COULDN'T BE HAPPIER with his crew.

Cara, Axe and Arenas, and him and Brick had taken out three major players in the Alamogordo drug scene thanks to information provided by Sheriff Nazarian. And while the drug thugs would be replaced, as always, the cartel wouldn't take the news of their sudden deaths well. Not when their refinery over the border was the next thing to go up in smoke.

Team Reaper, with fresh ammo and gear thanks to Roger Cross and his militia company, hiked in the dark through a notch in the mountains somewhere between White Sands and the city of Truth or Consequences. The team moved in a jagged formation, taking advantage of the natural cover, Kane leading the way. They were about to knock out the cartel refinery Nazarian had shown them on a map. Once that was knocked down, Arenas and Brick would depart for Mexico to try and get the Mexican First Lady on their side.

Stars blazed across the clear sky, the half-moon hanging over them. The team wore night vision goggles, and the starlight gave their head units ample light to magnify, the resulting green glow a view Kane had long become accustomed to.

His boots crunched quietly on the hard-packed ground as they moved through the notch, weapons at the ready, scanning for traps, ambush points, even drones the drug thugs might send out to view the area surrounding the refinery.

According to Nazarian, they were looking for a steel building with a water tower, both placed quietly in the middle of the nowhere outside Nazarian's jurisdiction where the Federal and State cops weren't looking, either by choice or bribe, Nazarian wasn't sure which. All he knew was that he'd complained about the refinery many times, and received no indication that anybody was attempting to solve the problem.

Team Reaper planned to solve the problem for good.

Without the helping hand of Team Bravo at HQ, Reaper was working without a net. They had no eyes in the sky. No chopper for infil and exfil. They'd left a pair of SUVs several miles back. Once they hit the refinery, they had a long walk back to the vehicles. If anybody was hurt in the fight, or didn't survive, they'd have a real long walk back to the vehicles.

Kane had attempted to contact General Jones for an update on Bravo prior to their departure, but Jones had been unreachable.

So they focused on the fight.

The best way to feel better about the situation was to kill some bad guys.

Kane and his crew spread out in a line, still using jagged rocks for cover, once they found the clearing where the processing plant resided. They almost didn't have to worry about making noise. There were enough rumbling noises from inside the steel building to mask their presence unless somebody saw them, and their night vision picked out several heat signatures around the perimeter.

Kane whispered into his com unit, "Ready with grenades."

He plucked one of his own high-explosive grenades from his web vest. He had no idea if the explosive would work. It was a home-brew built by the militia, and it looked like a rough copy of the old pineapple-style grenades used by the military.

If the locals could build that kind of ordnance, it made them a formidable force indeed.

Assuming the damn thing worked.

He pulled the pin and held the spoon tightly to the grenade.

"Aim for the water tower," Kane said, "and the center of the building."

Somebody will blow up something.

But if the grenades didn't work, they'd lose any element of surprise. The heat signatures of the sentries moved closer as the crew walked their assigned pattern.

The team whispered back one at a time: "Ready."

Kane tossed first, a forceful overhand throw for the base of the water tower. The grenade landed with a bounce, then skidded across the ground to stop under the tank. The wooden stilts and platform the tank rested upon appeared in the greenish night vision haze to be all wood, not metal. A little fire the blast might be nice.

Seconds passed and no boom.

Kane cursed.

Then the grenade detonated, the flash in Kane's goggles flaring, Kane turning away as the rest of the team lobbed their grenades. The intense detonations surprised Kane, and he traded a startled expression with Axe, nearest him. The militia had packed a lot of power into those pineapples.

The wooden stilts holding up the water tank splintered, the heavy tank falling as the supports crumbled.

The loud splash that followed as the tank split apart with a crash put out the small fires sparked by the blasts, and the steel building, with a big hole in the center now, was wide open for their assault.

Men yelling. Sentries converged on Team Reaper, Kane shouting for everybody to, "Let 'em have it," while grabbing another pineapple from his web vest.

He wanted to throw one right through the hole in the building.

Team Reaper opened fire, HK 416s crackling, night vision helping them find the incoming targets.

Kane gritted his teeth. Revenge felt good. He tossed the grenade.

CHAPTER 39

THE FIRST OF the approaching sentries fell spasmodically as 5.56mm rounds tore through them, their compatriots responding more tactically and hitting the deck to return fire. Rounds snapped over the heads of Team Reaper as they stayed low and behind cover and fired back.

Hot brass from Axe's HK fell on John Kane as he watched the second grenade sail through the opening in the building. Screams from inside, a few people running out. The blast lifted the building off its foundation, sending plumes of black smoke out the hole. Kane fired at the scattered drug technicians. Never mind they weren't armed; they were the ones refining raw material into poison. Kane dropped all three with well-placed shots, the HK barely kicking against his shoulder.

"Sentries down!" Cara shouted over the com unit.

Kane scanned the area, no more hostiles were in evidence. In the open, anyway. Some shooting from inside the building, as survivors tried to defend what was left, nicked at the rocks around them.

"Axe," Kane said, "get your bombs."

"Copy," Axe said, as Kane ordered the rest of the team to fire into the processing building.

No way were they venturing inside without protective gear. The burning raw drug material, and any finished product also on fire, would produce intoxicating fumes; they'd be breathing poison.

Axe had the unenviable position of placing plastic explosives around the base of the processing center. As the sporadic shooting continued, Axe removed his rucksack and shouldered his rifle. Within the rucksack, he had several blocks of C-4 provided by the militia. Nobody wanted to know where they'd collected the explosive material, but Axe had noted the '70s-era detonators that came with the bricks.

The gear might be old, but it still worked.

Axe belly-crawled across the rough ground. It wasn't comfortable. Sharp rocks bit through his BDUs but it was either that or get his head shot off by one of the drug thugs hidden in the building.

He hurried as fast as he could across the open space, finally gaining some cover when he reached the wrecked water tank and the remains of the wooden stilts. The ground was muddy; he slipped in the mud, digging the edges of his boots into the ground to move forward.

The shooters in the building couldn't see him now. He had a whole wall ahead of him, and his night-vision scan showed no openings for shooters to slip through. Based on the shooting, it didn't sound like there were that many to begin with.

Axe primed his first brick of C-4 and ran to the building.

Kane winced as a ricochet knocked rock dust into his left cheek. He fired another controlled burst into the building, but heard no reaction to the shots. For all he knew, they were wasting ammo and not hitting anybody inside.

"Reaper Four, Reaper One."

Axe calling.

"Go, Four!"

"Charges placed."

"Get to cover and let her rip."

"I'm on the north side behind rocks. Counting down from five..."

Kane, Cara, Brick and Arenas ceased fire and dropped to the ground. As Axe hit two, and then one, indignant gunshots still cracked from within the processing building. The shooters were quickly cut off when the trio of C-4 blasts sent fireballs moving swiftly from left-to-right across the interior, flames enveloping the walls, the roof falling, the ground shaking beneath the Reaper warriors. Scattered pieces of debris landed around them.

"Rally up and let's get out of here!" Kane shouted.

He trailed behind as his team ran, Axe catching up, the fighters heading off across the desolate landscape back to their vehicles.

The raid had gone without a hitch. Another check mark in the debt the drug thugs owed them for Team Bravo.

Very soon, Kane vowed as he ran, he'd have the kingpin in his sights. Or between his hands. The result would be the same.

———

Mexico City, Presidential Palace

First Lady Perlita Terrazas-Rojo didn't think her husband had her under surveillance. That meant she was more than likely free to speak in her bedroom without fear of video or audio recording, but she didn't want to assume anything.

As her assistant, Amaya, watched, Perlita turned up the radio, turned on the faucet in the bathroom, and gestured for her to follow to the balcony. Once the twin doors were shut, Perlita said, "We can talk now."

"What is happening, ma'am?" Amaya said. Butterflies had invaded her stomach. This was not a normal policy or scheduling discussion. Her eyes dropped to the balcony railing. It needed cleaning. A layer of dust sat on the top.

"I hate to do this to you, Amaya," the first lady began.

Amaya said, "What is it?"

"You are aware of what my husband is doing."

"Yes."

"I am not happy with what my husband is doing," Perlita said. "But there is no way for me to voice my opposition. I need help."

Amaya frowned. Was she being entrusted to help the first lady reach somebody outside the palace?

Perlita Terrazas-Rojo pulled a folded piece of paper from the pocket of her white jeans. She handed it to Amaya, who took it without hesitation. "The name of a reporter I trust. Go to him. Tell him that I am willing to talk and expose my husband's corruption."

The first lady's voice caught a little on the last two

words. But her expression remained stoic. She wasn't taking back the words. What had she found?

"You have...proof, ma'am?"

"I have what I need," the first lady replied. "Will you do this for me?"

"Of course, ma'am."

"Do you have a gun?"

Amaya started to answer but choked on the words. She managed, "No," and then the first lady said, "Follow me," and they went back into the bedroom with the loud radio and the running water. Perlita did not shut anything off. She went to a dresser, opening a top drawer and reaching well behind the drawer to remove a black automatic. A Beretta. She handed the gun to Amaya.

"Do you know how to use this?"

Amaya nodded.

"Keep it with you. You might need it."

"I hope not."

"So do I. Do not tell me when you're going, or if you contact him or not, just have him call me when he's ready to see me."

Amaya held the gun in both hands. "I won't let you down, ma'am."

Perlita smiled, but there was no light behind her eyes. It was a weak smile. A sad smile that suggested impending doom.

"I know."

CHAPTER 40

Presidential Palace, Rojo's Office

PRESIDENT ROJO FLUNG the digital recorder across the room. It struck the wall and split open, the pieces clattering onto the carpet.

"That won't change anything," said Federico Esteves.

Rojo leaned both hands on his desk and locked eyes with his number two. "Where did you put the bug?"

"Balcony railing. She checked around inside thoroughly, but not outside."

"What do we do?"

"I suggest we let your wife's chief of staff get off the property, then deal with her on the street and call it an unfortunate accident."

"And my wife?"

"Take her out of here. Perhaps to your cabin? Till further notice."

Rojo pressed his lips together. A red flush crawled up his neck.

"Do it," he ordered. "But do it quietly. Take care of the other one first. Baby steps, Federico. If we move too fast, she'll know something is up."

———

Mexico City

Amaya Olmos drove along Av Ruiz Cortinez and knew the blue sedan two cars behind her contained two men who wanted to kill her. It was the reason the first lady had given her the automatic. The President had made his bed with the drug cartels in a way that no other Mexican politician had ever done; what his wife was doing, and Amaya Olmos as her proxy, could not be allowed.

She'd spotted the blue sedan as soon as she passed the town limit, and had taken them on a winding tour of the city as she tried to ascertain whether they were truly following her. The blue sedan became as constant a companion as her nose.

She hoped it wasn't too late to help the first lady.

Amaya presently turned off Av Ruiz Cortinez onto Monterey, which wound through a housing tract on a slight incline. Down the block, the developers had left a cluster of hills and borders with a few trees here and there. If she had to face the goons in the sedan, she wanted them on her terms.

A glance in the rearview showed the sedan turning with her. No other cars on the road now. Just them. She slowed as she followed the curve of the road to the left, passing the hills, noting the mostly deserted homes. It was still mid-afternoon, and most of the occupants would be away.

She stomped the gas pedal. Her car lurched forward, tires screeching, as she finished the curve and stopped alongside the hills with a large fallen tree trunk a welcoming piece of cover. Jumping out of the vehicle, she pulled a Beretta Model 92FS from behind her back, the nine-millimeter with the checkered wood grips a comforting feeling as her shoes dug into the dirt. The grip was a little large for her hand, but she found the 15-round magazine capacity very reassuring. She headed for the trunk.

The blue sedan screeched to a stop at the bottom of the hill and the two men who climbed out carried submachine guns. They looked at her with hard eyes. Amaya felt a twinge of doubt. Her pistol wasn't much of a match for full-auto hardware. She dropped low and watched the two gunmen through a gap in the trunk. They started climbing, moving at a swift pace.

One of the gunmen stumbled and fell to one knee, putting a hand out to break the fall, and Amaya seized on the opportunity. She aimed the Beretta 92FS and fired twice. The sharp snaps of the rounds leaving the pistol echoed through the neighborhood. One bullet gouged the dirt near the gunman's hand, the other barely missed based on how the man dived into the earth. Amaya fired again, the round going wide as she tried to shift to the second shooter, but the trunk blocked the movement of the muzzle.

She moved quick, kicking up a small cloud of dust as she continued further up the hill to the top. Another tree trunk to her left exploded and shards of bark pelted her skin, the crackle of the submachine gun continuing as she rolled into the dirt and let the opposite slope carry her further away. Coming to a stop on her belly, she crawled behind a bush only to realize she had lost her pistol.

One look up the slope located the gun, in the middle of an open path, just lying there waiting for somebody to come and collect it. Amaya started to rise as the gunman appeared over the top of the hill. She dropped again. The gunmen spoke to each other rapidly, splitting up. One found the Beretta and jammed it in his belt. He started calling to her, telling her to come out from hiding and "take it like a woman", whatever that meant. Amaya had no need or desire to die this day. She watched through the bush as the shooter started down the slope to her spot.

She leaped out when he was within range and struck hard with a series of kicks and punches, including an elbow strike to the jaw which put the man down and out. She fell with him as his partner yelled, landing on her side and using the man's larger body as a shield. She grabbed his submachine gun. The second shooter ran toward them, his steps landing hard on the earth. She put the submachine gun's stock firmly to her shoulder, lined up the sights, and started to squeeze. The gunman stopped short, his eyes wide, clumsily bringing up his weapon to fire, but it was too late.

The weapon in Amaya's hands spat flame. She kept the trigger back, watching as the salvo split open the gunman's belly and spilled chucks of sticky red flesh all over the ground. The rounds shattered both arms, smacked into his chest, opening wounds, a bloody mist hanging in the air as the gunman dropped first to his knees, then toppled to one side. He slid along the slope until he came to a natural stop.

Breathless, Amaya jumped to her feet, tossing aside the now empty submachine gun. She retrieved the Beretta and put a round through the unconscious gunner's head, shuffling back to avoid the blood spray, but red spotted her shoes and pant legs anyway.

She ran. Back up and over the hill, hustling to her car. Diving behind the wheel, she left a trail of rubber on the asphalt as she executed a quick U-turn.

She didn't mind the blood spatter on her pants, but she needed a new pair of shoes.

As she drove, a new idea occurred to her. If the killers had known to look for her, and find her, perhaps they also knew where she was going and who she planned to see.

Which meant she needed to go see somebody else. While the first lady's idea about the reporter was a good one, the appearance of the killers meant they required a different approach.

She thought of an ex-boyfriend, a soldier, a man who was loyal to his country. Maybe she could trust him to help get to the reporter and get the first lady's plea for help to the world.

She needed to find a quiet place to pull over and get on her cell phone. Her heart raced not only from surviving the attack, but as she thought about what she'd tell Javier. She hadn't heard his voice in a long time.

CHAPTER 41

Washington, D.C., The White House, Oval Office

"FROM THE TOP, GENERAL," the president said.

President Jack Carter had only recently become used to talking to people over Skype. This time, he had General Jones of the Worldwide Drug Initiative on the computer. The laptop sat on the corner of Carter's desk, turned so not only could Carter see and hear General Jones, but also the three guests in the Oval Office.

The Seconds were back. Deputy Attorney General Grant Stockwell. Deputy DEA Director Alan Brinkley. Deputy CIA Anti-Drug Chief Steve Ransom.

General Jones didn't waste any time.

"Team Bravo is improving," the general said. "They've been moved from ICU into regular rooms and they're awake and talking. My people are taking copious notes."

"Very good," Carter said. He turned to the other three men. "What do you three have?"

Stockwell and Ransom had elected Alan Brinkley of the DEA to speak for the trio, all of whom had been hard at work gathering information and coming up with answers to present to the president at this meeting. Carter's orders had been clear. He wanted no stone unturned in the hunt for the killers who had invaded D.C. and El Paso and taken or damaged so many lives.

"Not much," Brinkley said.

Carter frowned. "I don't like that answer."

"What we have is only surface-level intel, sir," the DEA man said. "We've searched through thousands of minutes of traffic camera footage looking for the shooters who hit D.C., but none of it was helpful. Witnesses have been no help."

"So, all we know," the president said, "is that cartel killers infiltrated our country, killed our people, and left?"

"We don't think they've left, sir."

"Where are they, Alan?"

"We have people looking."

President Carter sighed in frustration. He turned to the image of General Jones on the laptop. "Where is Team Reaper, General?"

"New Mexico, sir, taking care of some issues there."

"Related to our problem?"

"I can't comment on what I haven't researched, sir."

"Aren't you talking to Kane?"

"My focus has been El Paso, sir."

"I want an update from Kane as soon as possible."

"I will get it for you, sir."

Carter didn't hide his frown any longer. "Gentlemen, I am not at all happy with these non-answers you've given me. I know you have people doing the best they can, but I have a public and a press demanding answers, and I need to provide them."

He snapped at Steve Ransom. "When will your people be on the ground in Mexico City?"

"We're coordinating with the Embassy people, sir. I don't plan on sending more down. We'll know in a few days if they're able to make contact."

Carter said nothing. He put his elbows on the desk and made a tent of his hands in front of his face. "Thank you, gentleman," he said.

The Seconds left the Oval Office. General Jones vanished from the laptop screen. President Carter sat quietly and stared at the wall in front of him.

The stress of the job never abated.

What he needed was a drink and a consultation with his wife. The first lady always knew how to listen, and he had a lot to sort out with her.

————

"We can't bluff forever."

Deputy Attorney General Grant Stockwell spat out the words as their limousine sped away from the White House.

He sat across from the other two men, both of whom wore an expression of worry.

"We need to find Team Reaper," said Brinkley. "Finish them off."

"Team Reaper is not the problem," Stockwell said. "The problem is we need a scapegoat. Somebody needs to take the fall for these killings, and Rojo and the cartels never planned to provide one."

"We need to tell them," said Steve Ransom, his voice low and even, "that they need to come across with something we can give the president."

"They're going to want to know about Reaper when we call them," Brinkley said. "We made promises."

"We have the hospital under surveillance," Stockwell said.

"Not enough, Grant," said Brinkley.

"We know they're in New Mexico," Ransom said. "If we dig a little, and see if anything is happening in that area, we might be able to find them very quickly, and trade the information for a patsy."

Stockwell let out a sigh and sat back heavily. "This deal gets worse all the time."

The stern expressions of Brinkley and Ransom more than confirmed Stockwell's observation.

The arrangement sounded good and profitable at the time. Sacrificing friends and colleagues in order to get into the top spots had been a risky move, but one they knew would pay off. It was the natural order of things until a new administration moved into the White House, but by then they'd have time to sink their roots deep into the establishment and make sure that, even when they were gone, their influence and ability to tap into the flow of information would continue.

They'd continue to wield power and earn money. Tons and tons of money.

It made the world go 'round after all.

And they might be doing a whole lot better if it weren't for Team Reaper. Kane and his crew were still alive; the El Paso headquarters personnel were too stubborn to die.

That had to change. Fast. Otherwise they'd have targets on their backs too.

There was always somebody else waiting to take over.

CHAPTER 42

South of the Mexico Border

"THIS IS A LOAD OF CRAP," Brick said.

Carlos Arenas chuckled. "It's my home, bro. Ain't no trouble for me."

"How long we been walking in the desert?"

"Long enough for you to get a tan!"

Arenas laughed again. Brick found no amusement in the remarks.

The Reaper duo wasn't dressed for combat. They carried only their SIG 9mm handguns, concealed under light windbreakers that looked out of place in the desert. Brick and Carlos were two wandering souls crossing a desolate region, hoping that the message sent ahead to Arenas' contacts in Mexico's Special Forces reached the right people.

Because if the note reached the wrong people, they were done for.

Per General Jones and his last contact with Team Reaper, Arenas and Brick were walking into Mexico to attempt to contact President Rojo's wife and see if they could get her cooperation in exposing her husband's new alliance with the cartels.

They hadn't expected her to contact them.

It almost happened like that, though, with the Mexican First Lady's assistant reaching out to her special forces soldier ex-boyfriend for help in the matter after two drug thugs tried to kill her.

Now, with the new arrangement and plan, Carlos and Brick were walking into Mexico where Sergeant Javier Gomez and his crew of shooters would meet them and help the pair get into Mexico City under the radar.

Because the first lady was ready to talk.

At least *half* their job was done.

Getting her into the United States without harm might not be as easy.

Brick wiped his sweaty forehead. He wore a hat to block out the intense assault of the sun, but it didn't matter much. Each of them carried a trio of canteens, and Brick had already drained one staying hydrated.

Several hours earlier, Kane and Cara have driven the pair as far south as possible, depositing Brick and Carlos at a point where the border was weakest, with no attention from the skeleton-crew Border Patrol still working the area. Nazarian had briefed them on the closed checkpoints and diversion of Border Patrol units to California, so walking through the open wound wasn't hard.

But it pained them both to see the US so vulnerable.

That had to change. Unfortunately, it was well outside their area of expertise. They could only focus on the task at hand and hope cooler heads in Washington eventually prevailed.

"Over there," Carlos said.

"We need cover."

Arenas concurred and they raced to a cluster of boulders and dropped into a squat. The thick dust cloud kicked up by the three vehicles concealed any markings or identifiable features. Arenas was sure it was Gomez and his crew but didn't want to take anything for granted. If they stayed in the open and the trucks belonged to cartel killers who had intercepted the coms between the US and Mexico, they'd be walking into their death.

Carlos was taking the lead on the mission, and Brick had no argument. Arenas, a ten-year veteran of the Mexican Special Forces prior to joining Team Reaper, knew the area best, as well as the shooters still loyal to the country who hadn't taken the bribes offered by the enemy, despite how lucrative they might have been.

Arenas swallowed. His throat felt dry, his stomach in knots. Brick took out his SIG.

"Easy," Arenas said.

"I can hear your knees knocking, Carlos."

"Yeah, well—"

Whatever pithy comeback Arenas had, vanished as the trio of trucks made a sweeping turn in front of them, kicking up more dust, the cloud sailing past the Reaper pair. The driver of one of the trucks rolled down his window and looked out.

"Hey, ugly! Come out from hiding!"

Arenas sighed in relief. "That's Javier. Put the piece away."

Brick returned the SIG-Sauer to shoulder leather and followed Arenas out from behind the rocks. The dust stung his eyes and he coughed. Arenas seemed unaffected and led the way to the trucks. Four armed shooters sat in the back of each vehicle, watching the two Reaper members closely.

The driver of the lead truck, though, was smiling and laughing. He jumped out and gave Arenas a hug.

"So, you've finally decided to come home!"

Arenas grinned. "Brick, Sergeant Gomez."

The special forces sergeant heartily shook hands with Brick and told them to get into the truck. He had room in the passenger cabin for both, but it was a tight squeeze.

Arenas, since he was smaller than Brick, sat in the middle.

As Gomez drove away, the other trucks keeping pace, Arenas said, "What's the score?"

"My ex came crawling back to me, like I knew she would someday," said Gomez. He was short and stocky but all muscle, the lines on his face a testimony to the stress of his job and the combat miles he'd logged over the years.

"Javier—"

"Hey, I gotta have a little fun with this, right? She told us what's going on and we put her in a safe house. That's where I'm taking you."

"What about the first lady?" Brick asked.

"She's been moved to the presidential retreat," Gomez said.

"Is that bad?" Brick said.

"It means her husband knows what's going on. They already tried to kill her assistant to keep her from talking, but they can't very well do that to the first lady. They're keeping her under wraps for now."

"But who's guarding the retreat?" Arenas said.

"That's the beautiful part, amigo. Normally government people are involved. Instead, President Rojo has given them a stand-down order, and replaced the crew with cartel shooters."

"That's *rich*," Brick said.

"We're going to have to bust her out of there, but at least we can kill the gunners and not lose any sleep, right?"

Arenas assured Gomez he'd lose no sleep whatsoever.

CHAPTER 43

THE RIDE TOOK two hours before Gomez stopped in an open area and ordered his men to spread out and establish a security perimeter. He explained that a chopper was on the way to take them to Mexico City where Amaya Olmos waited at a safe house.

The helicopter arrived on time, and Gomez climbed in with Brick and Arenas. The remainder of Gomez's crew drove the trucks out of the area.

After landing at a private airfield, Gomez changed out of his fatigues, keeping only his sidearm, and drove Brick and Arenas away in a compact sedan into Mexico City.

Sergeant Gomez stopped at the safehouse at Mercurio and Galaxia, where Brick noted they had easy access to a freeway. The quiet neighborhood seemed okay for the brief time they'd be there, but quiet didn't promise security. Brick and Arenas knew all too well that the nosy neighbors would take interest in the *gringo* going in and out of the house. Brick's skin color wasn't an advantage in this case.

Kids played down the block. More homes lined the street. Gomez said the house was used often enough for activity at the residence not to be out of the ordinary, but Brick's wary eye still scanned for danger, nonetheless. He didn't like being in a spot where civilians might be caught in a crossfire if a fight took place.

The front walkway led to a narrow outdoor hallway with the porch at the end. Gomez tapped a Morse code on the door before using his key. As a home, the interior was a joke. The door opened on the living room, which was bare except for a modest couch and folding chairs spread around the carpet. The dining room contained a poker table; the kitchen was at least stocked, and that's where they found two other men in the middle of a conversation, the pair Gomez had assigned to watch the first lady's assistant.

Arenas raised an eyebrow at the spartan conditions, but Brick reminded him that the house was a place to hide and nobody who spent any time within its walls was meant to stay there for very long. Gomez introduced them to the other two SF troopers, but they didn't stay long. Gomez dismissed them and they departed.

"Where's the woman?" Brick said.

Gomez called for Amaya, and she emerged from a bedroom down the hall. She looked nervous. Gomez introduced her to Brick and Arenas, and when Arenas assured her in her own language that they were there to help get the first lady to the United States where she could share her story, Amaya finally calmed down.

Arenas and Amaya sat on the couch to talk further while Brick and Gomez stayed back to listen.

Amaya told the story of her assignment and murder

attempt quickly, and Brick saw that the experience had shaken her deeply. She stuttered, shifted in her seat, and generally appeared uncomfortable with the whole situation. This wasn't what was supposed to happen in their country, she said. Arenas sympathized. Gomez watched her with sad eyes. He agreed. Their country was a mess and needed serious help.

Gomez brought Amaya Olmos some water and took Brick and Arenas into the dining room where Gomez had spread out a map on the poker table. Most of the map was draped over the edges of the too-small table. A red marking dotted the map near the coast in the Gulf of California.

"What do we have here?" Brick said. "The president's retreat?"

"Exactly." Gomez said.

"Do you have the manpower?" Brick said.

Gomez nodded. "The crew you saw me with when I picked you up is on the way. We'll be ready by nightfall."

"Who else knows about this?" Arenas said.

"A select few. We should be okay."

"Should isn't certain," Brick pointed out.

The front door exploded.

Two gunmen in commando garb and submachine guns held tightly to their shoulders stormed through the smoke and debris from the blasted doorway. They started scanning for targets, but the masks over their faces limited their vision, and that's all the time Carlos needed to shoot first.

The SIG 9mm in Arenas' fist cracked twice. One of the commandos dropped, almost colliding with his partner, who dodged, turning to fire as Gomez and Brick bolted for the kitchen and Arenas kicked over the poker table. The table would in no way stop a bullet, and the commando opened fire anyway, Arenas rolling away as the bullets tore through the tabletop and shredded the map. Arenas rolled onto his stomach, coming up with the SIG at eye-level. He fired twice again. The second commando jerked with the hits, but stayed on his feet, turning to run, diving for the couch. He leaped over the cushions, leaving a large red stain as he dropped over the side.

Amaya screamed and jumped up, running back down the hall. Nobody tried to stop her. Gomez ran after her, yelling commands.

The second gunman lifted his submachine gun over the back of the couch. Arenas, Brick now beside him, opened fire, dodging back toward the dining room only to trip on a chunk of the door that had landed on the carpet. Brick held onto the M-17 as his rear end slammed onto the carpet, but the commando saw the fall as an opportunity and shifted his aim. Brick rolled. The SMG's burst cut into the carpet where he'd been. Brick kept rolling but slammed to a stop against the turned over poker-table. He raised his pistol and fired at the couch, the slide locking back. The commando ducked back behind the couch. Brick and Arenas scrambled into the kitchen.

"We need bigger guns!" Brick said.

"Hell, we need a bazooka!"

Another blast shook the house.

"Back bedroom," Arenas said. He raised his voice hoping Gomez might hear. "More coming down the hall!"

The commando in the living room started shouting

in Spanish. Brick's ears were ringing from the gunshots; he couldn't quite hear the replies, but the voices indicated more armed gunmen were already inside and Gomez, holed up with Amaya, only had a pistol.

The enemy had them trapped in a kill box from which there might be no escape.

CHAPTER 44

BRICK GRIPPED HIS GUN TIGHTLY.

No way in hell were they going to die today.

More shouting in Spanish, the new voices louder, and Arenas shoved his pistol around the corner of the kitchen. He had a clear view of the hallway and the three new commandos moving in a staggered formation in the narrow space.

As Arenas squeezed the trigger, he wondered idly who ratted them out.

The SIG-Sauer M-17 cracked once, twice. The first 115-grain Winchester +P jacketed hollow point closed the distance between Arenas and his targets at 1335 feet-per-second and shattered the knee of the lead commando of the hallway team, the kneecap splitting in half and spilling a spray of red on the floor and carpet. The man let out a yell as he toppled forward, the second bullet striking him in the left shoulder as he landed. Arenas fired a third time, the 9mm stinger crashing through his ballistic helmet but containing the explosion of the man's head within. The blood spatter traveled downward, covering most of his face, and more of the carpet.

Arenas and Brick shifted their aim as the remaining pair of hallway commandos started to drop to one knee. As they raised their submachine guns, Brick let two more rounds go. They hit the second shooter high in the chest, knocking him off balance and backward. The commando fired a burst from his SMG into the ceiling, and plaster rained down, distracting the last shooter long enough for Arenas to put a single round through the man's chin. The bullet punched a small hole in front, jerked his head back as it traveled the rest of the way through, and exploded out the back with a shower of flesh, skull pieces, and helmet parts.

Brick slapped another magazine into the SIG and stood up, slowly working his way around the corner to deal with the last gunman still hiding behind the couch. The man was shouting, his words weak, as the blood loss from his wound more than likely began taking its toll. If Brick had been a humanitarian, he'd have gone over to assist the man. But he wasn't, so he crossed the carpet to the couch, stepped around, and settled the SIG's night sights on the cartel killer.

The man lay flat on his back, blood seeping into the carpet. He held up one hand in a "stop" gesture, his mouth still moving with words coming out that Brick didn't bother to try and understand.

Brick's finger tightened on the trigger once again and he shot the commando through the head.

———

The fight was over.

Arenas shouted for Gomez and Amaya, and the pair emerged from the hall, Gomez with his pistol at the ready.

"Nice work," the special-forces sergeant said.

"How far to your staging area?" Brick said.

"Two hours."

"We need to be there in fifteen minutes."

"I'll drive."

Gomez hustled Amaya outside with Brick and Arenas close behind.

There was no sign of cops.

"Strange, huh?" Brick said.

"Who tipped them off?" Arenas said. They climbed into the sedan. Amaya wasn't talking, but instead shaking from head to toe, her eyes wide with fear.

"I'll find the bastard later," Gomez voted. He put the car in gear and drove away.

As Sergeant Javier Gomez made a turn heading for the freeway, Arenas stole a glance down the block from the safe house. He didn't see any kids playing in the street any longer. He hoped they made it indoors before the bullets started flying.

Just another reason to destroy the cartels and everything they stood for.

————

Los Mochis, Mexico, Near the Gulf of California

Brick didn't like the idea of keeping Amaya Olmos with them but figured the first lady would want a friend close by when they pulled her out of the clutches of the cartel gunners.

The trucks were lined up with military precision.

Land Rovers, Hummers, Land Cruisers, and other large people movers sat in four rows in the desert, while troops milled about and prepared their gear.

Javier Gomez, Carlos Arenas, Brick Peters, Amaya Olmos and three squad leaders hovered over a map spread out on the hard ground, going over arrangements and discussing plans. A cloud of dust from footsteps and the arrival of the vehicles hung in the air; it was everywhere, causing itchy eyes and coughing.

They spent a half hour going over the area of the retreat and making plans. Arenas contacted Kane in New Mexico, who relayed word to General Jones that they were about to make a grab for President Rojo's wife. Kane called back to say Jones had arranged for extraction via the CIA, with no indication to Langley who their passengers would be, in Baja, California. Arenas promised they'd arrive on time.

"Are you ready?" Arenas asked Amaya once the meeting broke up.

Amaya had been issued an M-4 carbine like the rest of the crew, along with body armor, spare ammunition and grenades. She wasn't expected to join the fight. The weapons and gear were for self-defense only, and in the gravest extreme. The chest rig containing most of the combat accessories, looked too big on her frame, but she wasn't complaining.

"This fight needs to end tonight," she said. Her eyes looked beyond Arenas. Somewhere in the distance. Somewhere not where they were now.

When Gomez gave the signal, the special-forces

crew broke for their assigned vehicles. Engines rumbled to life. More dust filled the air as the vehicles moved out, splitting up in three directions.

Arenas, Brick and Amaya rode in the back of a Land Rover with Gomez up front, the driver navigating the memorized route to the presidential retreat.

CHAPTER 45

THE PRESIDENTIAL RETREAT sat on a flat piece of ground surrounded by green grass and a cluster of trees on the eastern side. On the opposite side, waves crashed against the shore.

The mansion was built in an L shape with a paved driveway at the 90-degree angle. From there, a brick path led to the front door.

Brick and Arenas, lying flat at the top of a hill, examined the layout through a pair of night vision binoculars. Amaya Olmos lay beside them. The uneven ground beneath him made the position uncomfortable, and Brick wanted to get into action straight away.

"You probably know every inch of that property," he said.

"I do," Amaya replied.

"Best way in from this side?"

"We're facing one of the garages. We can breach the door and get into the house that way."

"There's a lot of open ground to cover, though. The troops are going to see us. Why isn't there a wall?"

"President Rojo doesn't believe in walls."

"Really? I love a good wall. One that's a thousand feet high and has barbed wire on top."

"What are we talking about?"

"We're talking about getting your friend out of there."

"She'll be in the bedroom on the second floor of the west corner," Amaya said.

"Why?"

"The walls are reinforced to withstand bullets and explosions."

"So those walls are okay?"

"I'm not in the mood to be joking with you," Amaya said.

Brick cracked a grin.

"We just have to wait for Majors and the team to start the party." Arenas lowered the binoculars. "Then we go in."

Both were dressed in black. Amaya carried her borrowed M-4, combat accessories and a pistol. Brick and Arenas had their usual SIG M-17 pistols in shoulder leather and Mexican SF-issued Colt M933 carbines ready for action. An assortment of grenades hung on their chest webbing, M26 high explosive, smoke, and buckshot.

They heard the mortar rounds before they landed on the property, the tell-tale whistle overhead. Three high-explosive projectiles smashed into the ground outside the mansion, the explosions rocking the night, the flash from the blasts lighting up the area in a brief flare before the flames faded. More shells landed, not striking the structure itself, but the ground around it, and hopefully softening the resistance inside. By the time Gomez and his teams moved in, a swarm of bodies moving among the night shadows, the cartel troops had exited to meet the force head on, and automatic weapons fire crackled through the night.

"Let's go!" Carlos bolted down the hill with Amaya Olmos and Brick kicking up dust behind him. The cartel troops kept the fighting to the front of the house, the western side wide open to Brick and Arenas and Amaya's direct assault. The gunfire continued, getting louder the closer they came to the house, and Amaya took the lead. She moved along the wall to a door, tested the knob to find it locked, then fired one shot from the M-4 carbine to blow the lock and push through.

Brick and Arenas followed her into a darkened garage full of cars. Amaya hustled across the tiled floor, the rubber soles of their shoes squeaking as they moved.

"Are these cars all belonging to the president?" Arenas said.

"Yes," Amaya said. "Perlita only drives the Mercedes. Over there in the corner."

Arenas noted the white four-door Mercedes AMG S-63. They could use it to get to the extraction point.

Brick, Arenas and Amaya reached a second door, this one unlocked, and she pushed through with the M-4 tight to her shoulder. The Reaper pair followed, probing the dim hallway with the muzzles of the M933s.

The fighting continued outside.

———

Manny Valdes heard the explosions as he followed the access road to the presidential retreat.

He was the cartel man in charge of the force guarding the first lady, an odd assignment if there had ever been one. But orders were orders. If the woman wanted to talk to the Americans and ruin their arrangement with Rojo, he wasn't going to stop her.

He twisted the wheel and rumbled onto the shoulder of the road, a dust cloud surrounding the SUV, while he jumped out and grabbed an automatic rifle from the back seat. He ran around the back of the SUV to a rise, dropped, and watched. The mortar rounds exploded around the property, a swarm of soldiers rushing to meet the solid wall of cartel gunmen who erupted from inside. Battle sounds filled the night and Valdes knew it would be a slaughter. The assault force greatly outnumbered the cartel shooters.

Rage filled him.

The Americans had to be behind this. No mistake.

Valdes hefted the SIG-Sauer MCX rifle with the red dot scope and ran down the hill.

He had to get to the first lady and put a bullet in her. He'd explain later why. President Rojo would have to find a way to tell the public. That wasn't his concern. His concern was following orders and keeping Chucho Banderas happy.

He ran faster, his lungs burning, eyes stinging from the dust.

———

When the bombs started falling, Perlita Terrazas-Rojo crawled under the bed.

With each explosion, she cried a little. What was

happening? Why had she been thrust into this hell on earth?

Then gunfire. A lot of gunfire.

Was it the Americans or her own people coming to rescue her?

Her pulse quickened and she tried to control her breathing. All she could think about was getting away unhurt. If she hadn't been determined to spill the beans about her husband before, she sure was now.

Had the garage with the cars been hit? If not, she could conceivably get to the Mercedes and race away.

This was madness. This wasn't what she wanted. What had she done?

———

Amaya led Brick and Arenas up a flight of stairs to a hallway. She checked one side; they checked the other; all clear. They moved left down the hall. Amaya kept the M-4 tight to her shoulder.

She hoped she appeared confident to the Americans. She didn't feel confident. She didn't know how to use the weapons she'd been given, despite the brief lesson Gomez had provided. She felt vulnerable and she wasn't sure if she'd ever feel strong again after this. She wanted revenge against the cartel in general and Rojo in particular. How dare he bring them to this!

Her palms sweated on the grip of the M-4. Perlita's door was in sight. She held up a hand to signal Brick and Arenas to slow down and stop.

They had a knock code for such an emergency, she told them. Amaya used her left hand to tap the knock on the door.

One tap, two and three in quick succession, another tap, and two more spaced by three seconds.

"Ma'am, it's me," Amaya said.

Perlita Terrazas-Rojo's voice came through the door. "Who's with you?"

"Two Americans. Come on."

The door swung open. Perlita froze in the doorway. Amaya told her not to worry. "These men are friends. They're going to get us out of here."

The first lady said, "Then let's go. I have a car."

"And we have an extraction point," Arenas said. "Follow us."

Amaya took the lead once again, Brick and Arenas putting Perlita between them. Arenas took a quick scan of their six o'clock despite knowing no enemies could get at them that way.

Down the dark hallway. Back to the steps. Down the steps. Through a set of rooms where Amaya and Brick paused to shield Perlita from potential threats. Finally, into the garage, Arenas the last through the door as Perlita headed for the white Mercedes AMG.

Amaya shouted, "Get down!"

The M-4 popped. Manny Valdes, at the other end of the garage, dived to the floor and slid across to a red Ferrari. Amaya opened fire on the car, her salvo slamming into the bodywork and striking one of the front tires, the rubber blowing thunderously with the front end of the car sinking a little.

———

Brick fired in the direction Amaya indicated but didn't see the cartel man right away.

He fired on the Ferrari as well, both he and Amaya alternating bursts of fire. Brick shifted his aim to the next car in line, a make he didn't recognize right away, because it would be easy for Valdes to slither along the backsides of each car to reach their position.

The Mercedes rumbled to life. The headlights snapped on.

"Go!" Brick shouted.

Amaya bolted for the car while he provided covering fire, running his magazine dry and snapping in a reload as he dived into the back of the AMG. Perlita behind the wheel, Arenas in the passenger seat.

Amaya had the back window down and her M-4 poked through as they sped along the length of the garage to the exit. She fired blindly, with no sign of Valdes, but Brick hoped the shots kept him down long enough for them to get a head start.

"Hold on!" Perlita shouted.

The Mercedes crashed through the garage door, the thin metal bending to the will of the heavy car and breaking into several pieces. The car fishtailed a little, Perlita bringing it back in a straight line as she shot down the driveway to the access road.

Brick glanced out the back window at the fighting in front of the house. There was less shooting now, so maybe Gomez and his forces had the upper hand.

He hoped so.

———

Manny Valdes pushed up from the cold floor and ran for the nearest car, a bulletproof Lincoln MKZ, black in color, so it would blend into the night.

He put the SIG automatic rifle on the passenger seat and lowered the driver's side visor. The keys slipped from their hiding place and into the palm of his hand.

How hard was it to kill somebody?

Apparently *very* hard, once the Americans got involved.

The engine fired on the first twist of the key. Valdes put the car in gear and left a patch of rubber behind as the tires squealed beneath him.

He raced out the opening in the garage door, shaking his head. Such wanton destruction was simply uncalled for.

He steered the Lincoln down the access road, homing in on the Mercedes like a heat-seeking missile.

The battle would end. Here.

Tonight.

———

Amaya spotted the headlights behind them.

"He's behind us!"

Perlita shouted, "What's he driving?"

"The Lincoln!"

Perlita cursed. Amaya's face turned red.

"What's the problem?" Arenas said.

"Bulletproof."

"Shit," Arenas said.

"My thoughts exactly," Perlita replied.

CHAPTER 46

"WHY AREN'T we getting out of here with your main force?" Perlita said.

"Private extract for VIPs," Arenas said. "Safer that way."

"It can't be worse than Valdes coming after us," she said.

"Who is he?"

"Cartel thug. Scum of the earth."

"He's gaining on us!" Amaya shouted.

Perlita wrenched the wheel and the Mercedes screeched as she made a wide turn onto the main road, speeding up. The engine whined loudly.

"Are the Lincoln's tires bulletproof?" Brick said.

"Run-flats," Perlita said.

"This just keeps getting better," Brick said.

"Shoot the tires when he gets close," Arenas told him.

"Why is he going to get close?" Amaya said.

"Because if bullets can't stop the car, he'll use the car to ram us off the road."

"You were right about this getting better," Amaya said.

Brick plucked a grenade from his web harness. "You shoot, I'll toss this."

Amaya shoved a fresh magazine into M-4. "Read my mind."

"Plug your ears, kids," Brick said.

Brick and Amaya powered down the windows on their respective sides. Amaya leaned out with the M-4 and triggered three short bursts. Brick pulled the pin on the M26 fragmentation grenade and let the spoon fly. He pitched the grenade out the window, not haphazardly but aiming to keep the explosive on the roadway. If he could blow a hole in the asphalt and cause Valdes to wreck his car, his bulletproof machine would lose its value very fast.

The Composition B in the M26 detonated, a ball of orange fire erupting in the roadway with a thunderous crash.

The Lincoln swerved, going around the fireball, unaffected. The Lincoln swerved a little but quickly regained traction. The front end grew larger as Valdes pressed the throttle, trying to get closer to reduce the effectiveness of Brick's grenades.

The Team Reaper big man plucked another from his web gear and tossed, but too quickly. The grenade skidded across the lanes, off the side of the road, and the next blast only kicked up a pile of dirt.

Brick held back on his last M26 grenade. He still had buckshot and smoke charges but neither of those would be a defense against the big Lincoln. Sparks flashed on the road as Amaya's rounds impacted; Brick followed her lead and grabbed the Colt M933, but before he could pull the trigger, the Lincoln pounded into the Mercedes. The jolt made Brick grab for the passenger handle inside the car. The Lincoln backed off a bit, the Mercedes speeding up, the Lincoln powering forward to smash into the car again. Brick held tight but almost fell out the window. He let go of the M933, the weapon hanging by its sling around his chest and battering against his backside and used his other hand to pull himself back into the car.

————

If they wanted to get him with bombs, Manny Valdes had a way to deal with that.

He stepped on the gas. Not all the way to the floor, just enough for a surge of power and took him closer to the back end of the Mercedes AMG. He shifted slightly, aiming for the rear quarter panel. His heavy front end would make a hard impact and if he could hit the panel just right, the force would cause the Mercedes to spin out of control and then everybody inside would be at the mercy of his SIG-Sauer MCX and the .223 tumblers within its 30-round magazine.

Amaya Olmos was leaning out the window and shooting at his tires. How cute. She couldn't hit a damn thing with the wind smacking her in the face. She might score a hit eventually, but not before he scored the kind of hit he wanted.

He pressed the gas pedal a little more.

Closer.

He pounded into the Mercedes once, twice, smiling as he saw Brick nearly fall out the window on the right side, but Amaya Olmos held steady, as if planted in the doorway, her weapon wavering ever so slightly. He could almost look into her eyes, and what he saw scared him. She meant to kill him. As he started to back off just a bit, she fired. Flame flashed from the muzzle of the M-4 and the Lincoln shuddered as the front tire took the blast dead-on. There were run-flats on the wheels, yes; but they were not designed for the near triple-digit speed at which the Lincoln was traveling.

But he had to take the risk.

The front end swayed a little, Valdes correcting with the steering wheel. Foot on the gas. Bam! Into the Mercedes once again. Back off. Surge forward. Bam!

And then the Mercedes rear end slipped, the car beginning to fishtail as Valdes slammed into the rear quarter panel one more time. Rubber screeched as the Mercedes spun 360 degrees, across lanes, and off the road. The Lincoln flashed by, Valdes looking in his rearview. A large cloud of dust covered the Mercedes. It did not overturn, and they might make it back onto the road, but as Valdes slowed the Lincoln and powered through a U-turn to go back for the *coup de grace*, he knew he'd have to go all the way to take the option of escape away from them.

Which was fine. He was going to kill Perlita anyway. Amaya Olmos and the Americans were bonus kills.

Brick and Amaya collided with each other as the Mercedes left the road and bounced violently across the rough desert floor. Perlita screamed as she fought the wheel, and the loud clang that filled the car as it finally came to a stop told Brick that something had broken underneath and they weren't going anywhere anytime soon.

The engine stalled. Perlita pressed the starter again and again but nothing happened.

"We gotta get out!" Arenas shouted. The four piled out of the Mercedes.

The straining engine of the Lincoln drew nearer.

Brick looked around. The terrain wasn't flat. Hills, mounds, rocks, boulders, and plenty of bushes and trees.

Perlita stood with Amaya beside her, and Arenas told them to get to cover. Amaya grabbed the first lady's arm, shouting back at Arenas, "Make him go away!"

"With pleasure," Arenas said.

The Team Reaper pair checked their M933s and dashed around the front of the vehicle into open ground, weaving around boulders to a tree where he dropped prone just as the Lincoln skidded to a stop where the Mercedes had left the road.

Brick opened fire first, his rounds bouncing harmlessly off the body of the Lincoln before Valdes even exited. Brick thought Valdes might have time for a sandwich and let them use up their ammo.

But Valdes did exit and roll onto the asphalt, using the bulletproof sedan for excellent cover. They couldn't shoot through the car to get him. Either he or Arenas would have to get close. And that meant leaving their own cover and concealment to get at him face-to-face.

The odds were all in his favor.

———

Valdes clutched the SIG MCX close to his body as he sat against the driver's side of the Lincoln. A quick peek over the hood allowed him to see the two Americans behind the Mercedes. No sign of Perlita or Amaya Olmos. They must have spread out to try and create a crossfire.

So, two shooters to start, then only him and Perlita and Amaya. Easy pickings.

The Americans stopped firing.

They were waiting for him to do something.

He had the advantage and wasn't the only one to realize such a thing. He shifted onto his belly and crawled to the front of the car, stopping at the punctured tire. The white Mercedes sat still in the dirt. He could shoot through the car, but it wasn't a sure bet. The hard metal of the German car could deflect his bullets. But he had a better chance of hitting her than she had of hitting him.

He needed grenades. Why hadn't he packed any grenades?

You play the hand you're dealt.

And Valdes already held three aces and he was looking for the fourth.

———

Carlos Arenas thought he saw movement between the ground and the bottom of the Lincoln, but not enough for a shot.

He had another idea, though.

Arenas rolled onto his left side to take inventory of his grenades. The night's darkness didn't make it easy to see so he felt each one as it hung on his chest rig. One last M26 high explosive, one smoke, one buckshot.

Back on his belly, his mind quickly put a plan together. He'd have to carry it out without signaling Brick; in fact, he needed the big man to keep Valdes busy.

As if on cue, Valdes opened fire. His rounds smacked the Mercedes, punching through the metal, snapping off trim pieces, shattering windows. He was firing for effect, trying to scare them into the open. Brick returned fire. Arenas plucked the smoke grenade from his harness, pulled the pin, and pitched.

The grenade arced high before dropping solidly on the ground between the Lincoln and Mercedes. The grenade popped, thick smoke billowing from either end. The hiss overpowered the gunfire, and soon the shooting stopped as neither Brick nor Valdes had anything remotely resembling a target any longer.

The lack of wind kept the smoke cloud centered between the cars and Arenas took every advantage. He left the tree and circled around the edge of the cloud to drop prone directly in line with the Lincoln. Better, he was in line with Valdes's prone form at the front of the car.

The cartel thug must have sensed the movement, because he quickly rolled onto his back, brought around the muzzle of his automatic rifle and let a burst go as Arenas rolled left. The shots zipped by, audibly whistling as they sliced through the air, and Arenas answered with his compact carbine, the M933 bucking against his shoulder as the three-round burst left the muzzle.

The bullets struck Valdes's body with wet slaps,

punching through flesh and tumbling end-over-end as they plowed through bones and organs. Valdes screamed, his body tightening up and the rifle falling from his grasp.

Arenas rose to a knee, keeping his sights on Valdes.

"I got him, Brick!"

Before the words had even left his mouth, Brick ran around the front of the Lincoln. He paused a moment, almost enthralled with seeing Valdes's face twisted in agony, and he casually held the M933 at the hip and pulled the trigger until the weapon clicked empty. By the time that happened, Valdes was nothing of his former self. His corpse was a mass of open wounds leaking blood and turning the brown desert ground into a red-brown mud.

CHAPTER 47

New Mexico, Militia Safehouse

JOHN KANE STOOD in front of the wide living room window, looking out at the desert draped in a sheet of darkness. He felt like he was looking out into space.

Roger Cross and his militia squad were out on patrol, trying to determine if the cartels still had any trucks heading for the refinery they'd blown up. He wasn't certain word could have reached the cartels about the destruction, and it might be fun to see the look on the smuggler's faces when they realized they had nowhere to bring the product, but it was only a cursory concern.

His thoughts were mostly with Brick and Arenas.

He hadn't heard from them yet. Axe was monitoring the frequency they planned to use to check in, but the radio remained silent.

He glanced left where Axe sat at a table in front of a computer and speaker set standing by to receive Brick's coded transmission. He wasn't even sure the computer program was up to the task. It wasn't their standard issue means of such communication. They had none of their usual comforts on this job, and that reminded him all the more of Team Bravo, and whether they'd be able to ever rejoin the fight.

He hadn't bothered to look up what happened in El Paso because he didn't need his mind polluted with the idea that they might never totally recover.

And that was no way to think.

"Reaper," Axe called. "I got 'em, Reaper!"

Kane moved from the window to the table, sliding behind Axe's right shoulder to look at the monitor. Cara came over from where she'd been sitting, but Nazarian remained in his seat. The blonde deputy, Keely Lynton, had gone home a few hours earlier.

"What is he saying, Axe?" Cara said. She stood over Axe's other shoulder.

The monitor showed the waves of a sound file on the screen. Axe clicked his mouse at the beginning of the wave and pressed the space bar.

"Reaper Four to Strongbase One."

Kane shot a glance at Cara. The ridiculous name had been *her* idea.

"We've secured Missus Rojo and are proceeding to the extraction point. We should be back with you in a few hours. Out."

Axe stopped the playback. "Want to hear it again?"

"No," Kane said. He let out a sigh of relief. "It's good news and that's all that matters."

"We could use a little good news," Cara said.

"If the CIA people on that plane recognize her at all," Kane said, "they might start wondering what's up.

This could backfire very quickly if rumors start circulating."

"They're CIA, Reaper," Cara said. "They're trained to keep their mouths shut. They aren't going to talk about it over coffee."

Kane raised an eyebrow. "Wanna bet?"

She scoffed and returned to her seat on the couch. Nazarian watched curiously. Kane decided he'd better get the sheriff up to speed because, after all, he'd be helping with the security once Perlita Terrazas-Rojo reached American soil.

———

Alamogordo, White Sands Regional Airport

Kane and Cara handled the pick-up, meeting the CIA jet at White Sands near the same hangar they'd arrived at a few days earlier. Arenas seemed to have broken the ice with the Mexican First Lady, because she gravitated to him. Kane didn't interfere. After introducing him and Cara, they piled into an SUV for the trip back to the safe house.

Once there, they helped her get settled, showing her around, with Keely Lynton making a list of anything the first lady required to make her stay more comfortable. Kane gave her a rough outline of what they wanted from her. A statement, to start, and then more details on exactly what her husband and the cartels were up to, and what their future plans might call for.

She assured them she was ready to talk.

While Perlita Terrazas-Rojo spoke with Cara and

Deputy Lynton, Kane stepped outside into the fresh air to call General Jones.

"Good timing, Reaper," the general said. "I'm just about to visit General Thurston."

"How is she?"

"Awake and doing well. That goes for the rest of them, too. They'll be up and around in no time. We got lucky, Reaper. What's on your mind?"

Kane updated Jones, a weight leaving his shoulders with every word he spoke. The news from the general was exactly what he'd been hoping, praying, and waiting to hear.

"I'll make sure and tell her," Jones said. "Stay on alert. Rojo knows what's happened by now and he won't be happy."

"We have plenty of shooters here, sir."

"Where'd they come from?"

Kane grinned. "It's better I don't tell you."

Jones laughed. Kane did, too. It felt good to laugh.

El Paso, TX, Foundation Surgical Hospital

Mary Thurston's eyes opened slowly.

"How are you, Mary?"

The big figure of General Hank Jones stood on the left side of her bed.

"Is everybody alive?" she said. The words came out a whisper. She felt weak all over.

Jones nodded. "Everybody made it. It was rough, but everybody pulled through. Doctor Morales has been helping the other physicians whether they wanted her here or not."

Thurston smiled weakly. "Sounds like our doctor. What else is happening? Where's Reaper?"

"New Mexico."

"New *where?*"

Jones explained he diverted Team Reaper to New Mexico because of issues in Alamogordo, adding that he felt it wise to keep them on the road and in the field with the incidents taking place in El Paso and Washington, D.C. He told her of the killings of the attorney general, the DEA director, and the head of the CIA's anti-drug section.

"El Paso was no accident, was it?" she said.

"We believe all the attacks are coordinated." Jones further explained the suspected shenanigans between President Rojo in Mexico and the cartels, what they knew for sure from press conferences and phone calls from the Oval Office, and what they suspected.

"Has the world gone crazy?" Thurston said.

"More so than usual."

"Have you talked to Reaper today?"

"Yes. We successfully retrieved Rojo's wife from Mexico. She's going to tell us all she knows, and we're going to start a campaign to bring Rojo down. Make him resign. *Something* to reverse the policy they've implemented."

"If it stays the way it is, he's going to get a lot of people killed."

"You sound like your old self more and more every minute, Mary."

———

General Jones left Thurston's room and found a quiet table in the cafeteria. Thurston hadn't asked about the state of Reaper HQ, and he hadn't volunteered the information. She had enough to think about. There wasn't much news to report, anyway. The HQ property had been fenced off, sealed up, and repairs were already underway. The cover-up of what happened, and the official denials by public officials regarding the incident, was a trivial matter he'd let his people handle. They were the experts on that subject.

While he waited for his coffee to cool, he took out his secure cell phone. Time to update the president.

CHAPTER 48

White House, Oval Office

"I HAVE *some* good news to share," President Carter said.

Stockwell, Ransom, and Brinkley were all ears.

The president continued, starting with the update on Team Bravo as provided by General Jones, and then moving on to the extraction of Perlita Terrazas-Rojo from Mexico.

Stockwell reacted first to the news about the Mexican First Lady.

"We're going to get massacred in the press," he said.

"The press doesn't know about this, Grant," Carter said. "And since you're the only three people I'm telling, I'll know where the leak comes from if the press *does* find out, understand?"

Ransom, the CIA man, jumped in. "Rojo won't want this public, either, because then he'll have to explain what happened, or come up with a cover story nobody will believe once his wife's background gets into circulation. We might be able to exert pressure on Rojo without any statement from his wife. He'll know what she might say. Maybe we should approach him again."

Ransom ignored the sharp looks from his compatriots, though he understood their reaction. He turned to one, then the other, with no verbal comment. *We have to make it look like we're on the team, guys.*

Ransom turned back to the president. "What we need to do is get Missus Rojo *here*, to Washington, for her official statement."

"I agree," the president said.

"Where is she currently?"

"Undisclosed location," Carter said. "And that will remain the case until her arrival here in D.C." The president pointed at Ransom. "Steve, we'll need a CIA safehouse to stash her at. Can do?"

"No problem, sir," the CIA man said.

Presidential Palace, Mexico City

Federico Esteves regarded President Rojo without expression. The man was pacing, sweating, and breathing heavily.

"She wasn't supposed to do this!" Rojo said.

"Banderas and Zamorano aren't happy about the loss of their people," Esteves said.

Rojo stopped and glared at his number two. "Do you think I care what those two have to say on this?"

"You have to care. They're your partners. Like it or not. This isn't solely their problem to solve."

Rojo turned to look out the window at the bright

sunny day. Esteves gave him a few moments. Before he could speak again, Rojo turned around and squared his shoulders.

"What are we waiting for?" Rojo said.

"For Stockwell or one of the others to pass along the location of your wife, sir."

"They will risk exposure if they do."

"Part of the risk. One of them might have to take the fall."

Rojo nodded. "Federico," he said, "the Americans cannot keep her. As much as it pains me, Perlita will have to be sacrificed for the greater good of her country."

"Are you sure?"

"Yes."

"You understand that as soon as I call Banderas and tell him, he's going to send the team already in the US to deal with her."

"As soon as we find out where she is, I'd expect no less."

Esteves nodded and left the office. He returned to his own but didn't pick up the phone right away.

He knew why Rojo had given the order.

If he didn't contain the situation with Perlita, the cartel would cut their losses. Which meant they'd cut Rojo's throat.

Along with his own.

He and Rojo would be replaced by others whom the cartel might achieve better results from.

That couldn't happen. Perlita had to die.

———

Alamogordo, Militia Safehouse

Cara Billings joined John Kane on the porch of the cabin.

"How is she doing?" Kane said.

"She wants to know when she can start talking, and to whom," Cara said. "Bit of a fireball."

"Not surprised."

"I've been thinking."

"What?"

"With everything that's been happening, we can't trust that she'll reach Washington in one piece."

Kane, eyes in the distance, only nodded.

"I'd like to get her on video before she heads that way," Cara said.

Kane nodded. "That's fine."

"Cross says he has video equipment we can use."

"Tell him to bring it here."

"I already did," Cara said. She grinned.

Kane turned to her with half a smile on his own face. "How did you know I'd say yes?"

"Who knows you better than me?"

Kane let out half a laugh. "Sure. Get her ready to record and we'll put something on video ASAP."

Cara went back inside.

Kane sighed and glanced at the coffee cup still in his hand. It was empty. He set it aside.

Cara had a much stronger point than she realized. With Perlita Terrazas-Rojo in the US, she had a target on her back.

General Jones had already confirmed a helicopter pick-up. They weren't taking her to the airport. A special ops chopper would arrive at the cabin to collect.

Kane had a good laugh when Jones said that. A literal "black helicopter" was landing at a safe house used by the New Mexico militia. They'd love that.

He had to admit the unorthodox fighting crew was doing well. Since the destruction of the refinery, and the targeted killings in the city, drug traffic seemed to have slowed, as if the cartels needed time to regroup and plan their next move.

There had been some unusual "ultralight" activity over the desert, but Cross and his crew had no way to discern if the flights were from south of the border, so they'd let the craft pass. Perhaps the cartel was trying to get a 600-meter view of the area for strategy purposes, to find out where the US bushwhackers were hiding.

If Team Reaper in general and the US government in particular played their cards right, with Perlita Terrazas-Rojo's testimony, they could keep the bastards on the run for quite some time.

It was a lot of hope for, but Kane was working on being more optimistic. The war was everlasting, yeah, but sometimes a sliver of victory appeared over the horizon.

But only a sliver. Someday, maybe that sliver would get larger, and the war would be over for good, and Team Reaper would need to find honest work.

CHAPTER 49

THE CABIN WAS QUITE CROWDED.

Roger Cross, the militia commander, had posted the latest group of shooters rotating in around the perimeter of the cabin. Patrols and any interdiction activity were now cancelled. They had to make sure Mexico's first lady remained under protection until the special ops crew showed up to collect her.

Cross, having brought his home video equipment to the cabin, set up the small camera on a tripod, which he placed at the end of the dining table with Perlita Terrazas-Rojo at the opposite end of the table. She sat calmly, wearing clothes purchased earlier by Keely Lynton and Cara Billings, seemingly at ease with her surroundings.

Either that, or she concealed her emotions very well. Her eyes betrayed nothing of her thoughts; she sat stoically, waiting for her cue. Waiting to expose her husband's misdeeds as a way to avenge her fallen family.

Team Reaper, in full battle dress, remained inside

the cabin, positioned in front and in the rear of the house. Sheriff Nazarian and Deputy Lynton were in the city, tending to their various duties, and Nazarian expected to rejoin the crew that night.

Until then, it was only Kane, Cross, and their crews to see to Perlita Terrazas-Rojo.

Kane, Cara, and Axe covered the front of the house in the living room and front room, while Arenas and Brick took the back deck. Their com units were active and tied in with the militia members.

The chopper would arrive within an hour.

Roger Cross said, "Okay, we are ready."

Kane left his spot by the front window and stood behind the camera. Cross moved aside.

"Missus Rojo, please explain why you are giving this testimony today," Kane said.

She looked straight into the camera with no hesitation. Kane had to give her credit. She wasn't having any second thoughts. She'd made up her mind, and that was the end of consideration.

She straightened in the chair, looked into the camera, and began to speak.

"My name is Perlita Terrazas-Rojo, First Lady of Mexico. I am here to make a statement about my husband, Lucio, and his dealings with the cocaine cartels that have compromised my country and put millions of people at risk."

Kane listened as she continued with her story...

———

When the information on the cabin's location finally came, Diego Medina, aka *El Cortador*, rejoined. He and the big Russian, Boris Yakovlev, had been in New Mexico forever, it seemed, waiting for insight on where they needed to be. During the long wait, they'd heard of several targeted kills in Alamogordo, and the destruction of a refining center in the desert. They were chomping at the bit to get back into the fight, and the location of the cabin, and the quarry within, finally gave them the opportunity.

The 4x4 bounced over the rough terrain as the vehicle rolled cross-country, staying away from the main highway, heading for a spot away from the target where they could go in on foot.

The mission was simple. Kill everybody. Especially the woman, Terrazas-Rojo.

Medina couldn't help but ask questions about the target when the name had been provided, but Chucho Banderas hadn't provided a lot of information during their call. Instead, Medina began sending inquiries to friends across the border, checking news reports, and putting together what he figured was happening. When his people in Mexico confirmed the attack on the presidential retreat, he knew *exactly* why the first lady was in the US, and *exactly* what she was attempting to do.

She couldn't be allowed to succeed. Billions of dollars were at stake.

Medina glanced to his right. Yakovlev watched the screen of a portable radar device, the antenna for which was on the roof of the vehicle. His dark eyes were focused on a dot featured on the screen. Medina frowned and leaned closer.

"What is that?"

"Incoming."

"Ground or air?"

"Air. Probably a helicopter to pick up the first lady."

"Are we going to get there in time?"

Yakovlev laughed. "Of course."

Medina twisted in his seat, looking in the back-cargo area. One of the items, among the rest of their equipment, was a vintage LAW rocket launcher. The gear, supplied by cartel contacts, was enough for Medina, Yakovlev, and the team of cartel shooters already in the US and organized with a series of phone calls by cartel-leader Chucho Banderas himself.

The gunmen rode in a second 4x4, about 15-meters behind Medina's. Eight shooters, all experienced fighters, plus him and Yakovlev. The drivers would stay behind with the vehicles.

"How far out?"

"Another half hour at least," the Russian said.

To the driver, Median said, "How much longer?"

"Fifteen minutes to the staging point."

"Okay," the Cutter said.

They could knock down that incoming chopper. No problem.

The 4x4 continued on its way.

———

John Kane called General Hank Jones on the sat phone.

"What are you going to do with the video?" Jones said.

"Axe is processing the footage right now, on a laptop. He's going to upload it to his cloud account and provide the password. He says to ignore everything in his account except for the file with the first lady's name on it."

Jones laughed. "I shouldn't be surprised, should I?" It was a statement, not a question, and a moment of levity Kane was happy to share.

"We appreciate the updates on Bravo, sir," Kane said.

"Of course. I wish I could say this was almost over, but we really aren't sure what we're in for, this time."

"We're going to end it one way or another, General," Kane said. "Count on it."

CHAPTER 50

KANE HELD binoculars to the sky but saw no sign of the expected Black Hawk. As he lowered the binos, he spotted something that didn't belong.

The ground in front of the cabin sloped down slightly, enough that Kane had to control his advance to a nearby tree for cover, and a better look.

He knew they weren't far from a freeway but seeing any part of a vehicle at this time set off his internal alarm bells.

He looked through the binos again. Sure enough, partially concealed maybe 200 yards away, was the back of a 4x4, the make and model of which eluded him, but it didn't belong there. His inspection also picked up the gouges in the ground made by the tires.

Off-roaders? Possibly. He swept the area but didn't spot any people. That's what really set him off. Anybody coming out to tear up the landscape and party would be whooping and hollering. At least they'd be *visible*.

Kane lowered the binoculars and retreated into the

house. He called for his team and Roger Cross to join him in the living room.

"What is it, Reaper?" Arenas said.

"We might have hostiles about two hundred yards away."

"Waiting for the chopper?" Cara said.

"Waiting for anything," Kane said. "Who knows? All I know is we have a high-value target to protect, and we need to get a closer look at what's out there."

Roger Cross said, "Let my people check it out."

"Too risky."

"You're going out there kitted out like a soldier?" Cross said. "My guys look and dress like locals. They can scout and see what's there."

Kane nodded. "All right. But tell them to be careful. I don't like involving civilians as it is."

Cross left the room to retrieve Billy Trache and another militiaman named Hammond from the back deck. Kane had gotten to know Trache a little and considered him a sharp chap indeed. Especially with a long-range rifle. If there was a civilian shooter who could give professional shooters a run for their money, it was Trache. But he was still a civilian. Yeah, he'd volunteered. Sure, he knew the land. But it was outside of Kane's comfort zone to send him.

Kane explained the situation, and Trache and Hammond grabbed their gear to take a look. Kane told them not to get within 50 yards and if they saw hostiles to radio back. He told the rest of his crew to get ready. If the cartel was planning to attack, they had to keep the enemy occupied until the Black Hawk showed up.

"How do they know we're here, Reaper?" Brick said.

"Good question, Brick. I'm not sure what the answer is."

Kane grabbed his pack and weapon. There was a second part to his answer he kept to himself. *But I'm going to for sure find out.*

———

The two militiamen, Trache and Hammond, dressed in street clothes with proper hiking boots and heavy coats to defeat the chill, clutched AR-15 rifles close as they moved through the wooded terrain, crunching fallen pine needles and tree bark as they moved, to a high spot where they might get a better look at the truck Kane had spotted. They weren't afraid of making some noise at the present distance. If the party in question were indeed off-roaders taking a break, there was no harm. If not, they'd know soon enough.

Trache and Hammond communicated with hand signals, Hammond splitting off to the left while Trache dropped behind a hollow log and took out a pair of binoculars. He scanned the area, wishing he could see through the trees, but the rolling terrain showed more than required. The land wasn't right. He counted several mounds that might have been camouflaged gunmen.

He started to signal Hammond with a chirping whistle but that's when a bullet ripped into his chest.

The shot came from one of the unusual land formations, from the snout of a barrel protruding from a camo net matching the browns of the forest floor. Trache let out a short scream, cut off because of the blood filling his throat, but his right finger twitched on the trigger of his AR-15 as he felt. The semi-automatic weapon snapped once, a bullet chunking into a neighboring tree, and then Trache fell flat and didn't move.

Hammond, a few years younger than Trache, knew when to boogie. He dropped into a crouch and shouldered his rifle, firing rapidly in a random pattern, before bolting to the right, taking advantage of trees and a boulder for cover as he worked his way up the slope for the long way back to the cabin. No doubt they'd already heard the shots, but he grabbed the portable radio from his belt anyway.

"We're taking fire! Billy's down! Billy's down!"

"Where are you?" Cross said over the speaker.

"Running up the hill to come around the back side of the cabin, don't shoot me."

"Location?"

"Hundred fifty yards east of the cabin." Hammond breathed heavily as he ran.

"Kane said two hundred yards."

"They're getting closer, boss," Hammond said. He kept running. No shooting behind him; either the enemy couldn't see him, or they were shifting their own positions.

A feeling told Hammond that he hadn't scared them away. Not at all. They were here for a fight and were going to stick around until the last bullet.

———

News of Trache's murder spread through the cabin quickly, the remaining militiamen eager to go out for revenge, but brought under control by Roger Cross who told them the worst thing they could do was run out and get cut down. They had a VIP to protect. He wanted everybody dug in around the house in the pre-arranged defensive positions, where they'd be joined by members of Team Reaper.

Kane called Sheriff Nazarian and advised him of the incoming attack, asking for whatever backup he could provide. Nazarian promised to respond with helicopters and the county SWAT team.

Kane raised the Black Hawk on the sat com. The chopper was ten minutes away. Kane told them they were flying into a trap, because the enemy wouldn't be able to resist such a juicy target. The Black Hawk crew chief assured him they had a crew of special ops shooters ready for a fight.

CHAPTER 51

KANE SPOTTED the incoming Black Hawk.

"Captain," Kane told the pilot as he consulted his GPS unit, "I suggest an alternate landing point about fifty clicks east of here. We'll move the VIP from this location and meet you there."

Kane looked out the front window of the cabin, where the chopper was now visible in the distance. The aircraft began to turn. "Copy, what am I looking for?"

"A flatter area than we can provide and somewhere further away from—"

The rear of the Black Hawk exploded as a fiery contrail left the forest floor. A portion of the rear tail section separated from the Black Hawk, and the chopper began a slow pitch downward. Kane didn't bother yelling for the captain. The man now had his hands full. The chopper disappeared below the tree line and then the ground shook from the crash.

Kane spoke into his com unit. "Brace for attack, they're coming." He felt for the safety of his HK 416 to make sure it was "off".

"Reaper!" Brick said from his position outside. "We got incoming!"

Before the Team Reaper big man finished the sentence, automatic weapons fire began chattering outside, stray rounds nicking the outside of the cabin, cracking the front window.

Kane left the living room for a spot down the hall where Cara had Perlita Terrazas-Rojo sheltered. They were on the floor, away from a window, a bed between them. The bedroom was quite spartan, but it wasn't like a full canopy bed and sculpted headboard was required at a time like this. Kane stopped in the doorway.

"This is it," he said.

"Copy," Cara said.

The Mexican First Lady yelled, "Kill them all!"

"You'll fit in perfectly here, ma'am," Kane said. He grabbed his cell to quickly call Nazarian to see about his estimated arrival time.

They were going to need all the help they could get, and fast.

———

Boris Yakovlev, a LAW rocket on his shoulder, put the crosshairs of the weapon ahead of the Black Hawk helicopter's nose. When the rocket flashed from the tube in a blaze of fire and smoke, Diego Medina whistled for the rest of the troops to begin their advancement on the cabin. They already had their orders. When the chopper crashed, open up.

Two teams of four, three men with automatic rifles and one with a heavy machinegun in each team, ran

through the woods to the cabin, their forest camouflaged uniforms making them a blur against the terrain.

"Down she goes!" Yakovlev announced.

Medina looked to see half the Black Hawk heading
for the ground. The thud and boom of the crash
followed within seconds.

"You aimed for the nose," Medina said.

The big Russian tossed the empty LAW tube onto
the ground. "A hit is a hit."

Then shooting started at the cabin.

Medina and Yakovlev checked their Kalashnikov
AK-12s and ran to join the fight. They had their own
mission: get into the cabin, kill Mrs. Rojo, then kill
whoever stood in the way of their escape. Their run
started up a slope, neither breathing hard, Medina
focused solely on his tasks. He didn't want to let the
cartel down. A lot was riding on his reputation. The
Rojo kill would be a feather in his cap and make him a
legend among killers. A bigger legend than he'd already
become.

He tasted victory, and that made him smile as he
ran faster.

———

The rest of Team Reaper and the militiamen were dug
in on the west side of the house, the short pits dug in a
crescent around the house, since that's the direction the
enemy was coming from. The stream of auto fire from
the forest brought everybody to attention, Brick, at the
forward-most pit, shouting for everybody to carefully
select their targets because the enemy was concealed
enough for their forms not to be obvious.

Brick, his HK 416 propped in the dirt, his head up high enough only to look through the IR sights, triggered short full-auto bursts while the two militiamen beside him fired single shots. Their AR rifles had no full-auto capability, but at least they shared ammo should somebody run low.

The cartel force looked small from what little movement Brick saw, and he radioed the information to the rest of Reaper, Axe with his two militia partners in one pit, and Arenas with his pair, which included Roger Cross, in another. He hoped Kane and Cara in the house had a handle on the Mexican First Lady. If not, the mission was for naught.

And with the Black Hawk gone, they were simply waiting for Sheriff Nazarian and his SWAT team.

If they could hold out that long.

Movement. Brick fired without hesitation. The HK kicked against his shoulder, the full-auto burst leaving the barrel with a flash of flame. A body fell, knocking aside part of a log that concealed another cartel shooter. The militiamen beside Brick aimed at the new target. Their rifles cracked. The target moved back, the log splintering with hits.

Brick ducked under the rim of the pit and spoke into his com unit.

"We need some grenades, now!"

"They aren't close enough, Reaper Five!" Axe said.

"From where I'm sitting, they're gettin' close!"

Brick grabbed a grenade from his web belt, one of the home brew pineapples the militiamen had distributed, saying, "This shit better work," as he pulled the pin and executed a perfect overhand toss. The militiamen covered him, firing as fast as their trigger fingers allowed as Brick grabbed his HK again.

The grenade blast shook the ground, a flash of flame engulfing some smaller trees, knocking one over, exposing two cartel shooters who cried out as shrapnel ripped through them.

Brick's smile of satisfaction didn't last long.

Because then the heavy machine gun started.

CHAPTER 52

AXE WATCHED Brick toss the grenade. He clenched his teeth. The home-made bombs had worked during the raid on the refinery, but would all of them work? The grenade did work, and not only took out the pair behind a tree but forced another to move from cover. Axe took the shot, a short full-auto burst, stitching the cartel shooter from hip to shoulder. He tumbled to the ground, trying to crawl. Axe fired again, missing, the shots ripping through ground foliage instead.

The shooter crawled out of sight.

Two more cartel shooters separated from the main group, running fast up the incline, both carrying RPK-16 with what looked like drum magazines. That meant 96-rounds of 5.45x39mm projectiles were coming their way.

Axe shouted the warning. "Two machine gunners breaking off!"

His words were drowned out as the first machine gunner dropped prone, his weapon propped on a bipod, and the first salvo of rounds hammered at them.

Axe dropped, pulling at the militiaman close to him to get him to duck, but not fast enough to grab the third man. Part of the salvo smacked flesh and the citizen soldier fell back, crumpling awkwardly at the bottom of the pit.

"Can't help him now!" Axe shouted to the survivor, who nodded, rising to return fire with Axe. Both their weapons barked. The machine gunner rolled away as the shots kicked up debris where he'd been.

The second RPK gunner swept a salvo across the pits, the sharp chirps of overhead passing rounds letting everybody know how close he was.

Time for a grenade of my own.

Axe grabbed and tossed it as hard as he could. The resulting blast kicked up enough dirt to leave a crater in the ground, but it satisfied him to see part of the second RPK gunner's body in the hole.

More assault rifle fire came their way as the troops in the forest advanced further.

We'll be hand-to-hand any second!

Axe slapped a new magazine into his HK and opened up again.

————

Yakovlev and Medina dropped flat when the big Russian shouted that he saw a grenade.

The detonation wasn't near them, but they felt the shockwave of the blast. They'd gone far enough up the incline where they were, perhaps, 50 yards from the fighting, out of sight of the cabin defenders as well as their own troops. The risk of being shot by a stray round fired by one of their own people was high, but the risk wasn't as great as the reward if they accomplished the mission.

Chucho Banderas and Victor Zamorano had promised to triple their fees should the Mexican First Lady not survive her stay in the United States.

Yakovlev shouted an alarm as two Americans met them at the top of the rise looking down on the cabin. Their civilian rifles and clothing marked them as not professional soldiers. Medina wondered who they were actually fighting as he and the big Russian turned them into Swiss cheese with their Kalashnikovs. Running around the bodies like they weren't any more bothersome than a fly in a kitchen, they started their approach to the rear of the cabin.

Both dropped behind cover to observe. Rear deck, rear sliding doors. No sign of further defenders.

Medina plucked a grenade from his webbing. "Let's announce our arrival and see if anybody's back there," he said.

Yakovlev readied his rifle.

———

The grenade blast rocked the cabin.

"Keep her down, Cara!" Kane shouted as he pivoted in the direction of the blast. It came from the rear deck, to Kane's left as he stood in the doorway, and the shattered patio door glass and small fires on the carpet told him somebody was coming through the back after having already broken through the rear defense.

"Reaper One," Kane said, "to everybody. They're coming in the back of the house, repeat, they've breached the house."

The last three words came out in a rush as two men, one large and the other slightly smaller, but both clutching Kalashnikov AK-12 rifles, charged across the damaged deck and through the gaping hole where the patio doors had been.

Kane fired as the men dived for cover, one rolling into the kitchen right of the back deck, the other heading left to the dining room. Kane's full-auto burst missed both.

Across Kane was the open floor of the living room with its various obstacles that could provide cover; getting out through the front, into the waiting hail of bullets of the forest assault force, wasn't something Kane was keen on attempting.

If only the Black Hawk had made it...

If only Nazarian and his SWAT force would arrive...

Focus!

This wasn't the time for what ifs. Kane had to deal with the here and now and that meant the two shooters currently attempting to engage him to get to Perlita Terrazas-Rojo.

He had to stop them.

"What do we got!" Cara shouted behind him.

"Two dudes with AKs."

In Kane's ear, Arenas said, "Reaper One, Reaper Three."

"Go!"

"We can assist if you need it!"

"Negative, Reaper Three, stay there!"

A sliver of movement in the kitchen. Kane fired a burst, the shots not hitting anything human but tearing up various fixtures. Kane shifted his aim to the dining room. Another burst. Whoever was there crawled further into a corner.

Kane grabbed for a grenade. An underhand toss sent the pineapple flying toward the wall next to the wrecked patio doors. It hit was wall solidly, bouncing off and flying into the center of the kitchen. Somebody screamed. Kane ducked back. The ensuing blast destroyed what remained of the kitchen and anybody on the floor.

They're going to wish they never started this!

Kane slapped a fresh magazine into his HK and said, "Get her under the bed. There's only one left and I'm taking him out!"

Cara acknowledged and helped Perlita Terrazas-Rojo slide under the bed. She was petite enough to fit. Cara snapped her HK to the ready position. Kane left the doorway.

CHAPTER 53

MEDINA COVERED his face with his left arm as the grenade in the kitchen exploded. The big Russian let out a short scream, cut off as the blast ripped his body apart. Poor bastard never had a chance. He'd been a good fighter, though, and as *El Cortador* lowered his arm and gripped his AK, he swore vengeance for his Ruskie compatriot.

The American ran out of the doorway. An odd choice. If he was guarding the Rojo woman, he was leaving her exposed.

Well, Medina wasn't going to let such an opportunity go to waste.

He ran out from behind the dining table chairs with the AK spitting flame.

———

Kane fired one round as his opponent revealed himself, and then dived into a somersault as the AK-12 let rip. Scrambling behind a couch, the bullets slammed into the back, destroying the cushions. As stuff flew around him, Kane aimed through the space under the couch. At the other man's feet. The HK 416 spoke once, twice, the 5.56mm tumblers quickly closing the distance, but his aim was off. One of the table legs splintered, the other smacked into the wall behind the man.

Kane rose to one knee, the HK shouldered now, firing again as the cartel killer dived forward, sliding across the wood floor. He reached the back of the couch and jumped over it with a loud yell, crashing headlong into Kane.

Both men fell onto the wooden coffee table behind Reaper One, the solid oak holding as they collided, rolling off with Kane on top of the other man. He swung the butt of the HK for the man's face, but the cartel killer blocked with the stock of the Kalashnikov, moving a knee between them and forcing Kane off with a loud grunt.

Kane fell back hard, the HK sling tangling around him. As Kane pushed the weapon out, the other man tossed aside his weapon and grabbed for a gleaming stainless-steel knife. He dived. Kane fired and missed, the bullet singeing the man's ear. Kane rolled away as the killer hit the floor. He tossed the HK and grabbed for his pistol, thrusting it forward, only for that gleaming knife to flash through the air and nearly slice through Kane's right arm, the blade continuing to thud solidly into the wall behind.

Kane screamed, the gun falling from his finger as sharp pain raced through his arm. *Two can play at this!* He grabbed his own knife and charged at the cartel killer as the man drew another and met the lunge with the solid block of his free arm.

Kane jabbed, the other man dodging to the side, Kane shuffling back as the other man slashed with his blade. The pair circled each other for a moment, Cara yelling for him to move out of the way. Kane yelled back: "Stay with the woman!"

The other man lunged, executing an upstroke that Kane parried with a counter-stroke, the blades clashing, both men scrambling apart to face each other again.

"They call me *The Cutter*," the other man said. He laughed. "You are no match for me."

"And they call me *Reaper*," Kane said. "You're about to find out why."

The Cutter laughed again. Kane charged, blade forward, tearing at the Cutter's left sleeve as he blocked, the other man grunting as the blade met flesh.

Medina kicked Kane in the stomach. As Kane doubled over, Medina lunged, bringing the knife up in an arc. Kane pushed forward on his right foot, slamming Medina in the gut. They landed on the floor again, knife strikes blocked by fast-moving arms, Kane using a momentary opening to smack Medina in the face.

Medina screamed, slashing, Kane feeling sharp pain in his face and neck as the blade scored, backing away before any killing blow could be achieved.

Medina jumped up, grabbed a third knife from his belt. His eyes flashed to the bedroom doorway, and his right arm flashed, the first blade leaving his hand and sailing into the room. Kane executed a perfect backspin kick, the heel of his boot meeting Medina's chin, but the Cutter only recoiled back and did not fall. They charged each other, Kane wincing as the second knife passed close to his belly, Medina's arm extending behind Kane's back. That's all it took. Kane drew his arm back and thrust forward.

The blade slammed into Medina's upper chest, only to meet the resistance of body armor. Before he could recover, Medina brought a knee up to Kane's groin and scored.

Kane stumbled, falling back into furniture, tumbling over a chair. He landed next to his SIG M-17. As Medina moved in, Kane rolled to the right, grabbing the pistol with his left hand. He bumped into the couch with his back exposed. Medina landed hard on top of Kane and brought the knife up.

Two blasts from Cara's HK filled the room. Kane twisted around and saw what remained of the stunned expression on Medina's face. Most of his face and neck was a bloody red mess, torn apart by the steel-core 5.56mm stingers in Cara's HK 416.

Kane shoved the body off him. Medina hit the floor with finality. He did not move again.

Kane said, "I had him!"

"She's dead, Reaper."

Kane jumped to his feet and ran to the doorway. His mouth dropped open all pain forgotten.

Perlite Terrazas-Rojo lay on the floor, the knife Medina had thrown jutting out of her throat.

"She popped her head up to see what was going on," Cara said. "Before I could stop her—"

She stopped talking as Kane went to the body. The knife had gone through her neck, the point protruding out the back.

Stunned, Kane sat down. He let out a long breath.

The battle continued outside.

CHAPTER 54

BRICK and the remaining militiaman in his pit opened fire on the charging cartel gunners, some of whom fell to not only their fire but others, the RPK-16 hammering somewhere off to the left.

"This is Reaper," Kane said over the com unit. "We're coming out!"

Brick didn't respond as he sent full-auto bursts into the on-rushing shooters.

Kane and Cara raced out of the cabin, stopping at the front deck to join the fight, their HKs spitting fire. More gunners fell.

"We're pinned down!" Axe shouted over the com unit.

Kane and Cara ran to the end of the deck on their left side, the RPK-16 turning their way, rounds chewing up the railing and the side of the house.

Kane dropped flat, firing through the gaps in the rail support beams, Cara taking her time as she sighted through the IR sight and let a round go.

The top of the heavy machine gunner's head

exploded. The man dropped flat beside his smoking weapon.

The firing ceased.

"Civilians, maintain your positions," Kane said. "Team Reaper, mop up."

Kane and Cara leaped over the rail onto the ground, joining with Brick, Axe, and Arenas as they ran to the bodies of the cartel troops, confirmed the dead, and ran into the forest.

Three gunners were already running away. Kane fired in their direction yelled for his team to pursue.

Team Reaper didn't require the order.

The five warriors gave chase, driven by vengeance for what had been done to their friends and colleagues in El Paso. It wasn't the exact revenge they wanted. They really wanted the ones responsible. But the three troopers trying to escape would suffice.

For now.

Arenas sprinted past Kane, cutting left, going for high ground. He aimed ahead of the three and loosed a burst. Ground churned up in front of the men. They stopped, scattering, one returning fire only to drop from a burst fired from Brick's HK.

Kane charged toward one target, a stocky man hurriedly reloading his rifle. Kane reached him before the magazine was fully inserted and blasted two rounds through his chest. The man's body flopped on the forest floor.

Another trio of pops signaled the demise of the last gunner.

Cara's voice on the com unit confirmed.

"All clear."

"Back to the cabin," Kane ordered.

By the time they returned, Roger Cross, Hammond, and the rest of the surviving militiamen had gathered on the deck. Their faces were dirty, clothes torn, weapons held aloft. They looked like soldiers. Kane patted Cross on the shoulder. "Good work."

Cross' voice almost broke as he said, "We lost four."

"I'm sorry. They'll be taken care of."

"I have no doubt about that, Reaper."

Cross shook Kane's hand.

Sirens in the distance grew louder with the passing seconds.

Sheriff Nazarian, arriving with the cavalry.

Kane looked around at the carnage.

Better late than never, but with a hell of a price to pay.

———

Washington, D.C., The White House, Oval Office

It was a somber meeting that didn't last long. When Stockwell, Brinkley, and Ransom had departed, only General Hank Jones and President Jack Carter remained in the Oval Office.

Carter sat behind his desk with his head in his hands. He looked up at Jones.

"We have the video," he stated.

Jones, standing before the desk, hands behind his back, said, "Yes."

"We can use that as leverage."

"We can indeed."

"But?"

"There's a leak, sir. How did the enemy know where to go?"

Carter said nothing.

"Who else knew about the cabin, sir?"

Carter said, "Me. You. Team Reaper."

"And?"

"The three men who just departed this office."

"Are you thinking what I'm thinking?"

"Raids against Reaper, a series of murders here in D.C.—"

"A plot to put people friendly to the cartel and Rojo's policy in charge, sir."

Carter nodded. All color drained from his face.

"I think you're right."

"The question is what we do about it."

"I'm open to suggestions."

"I suggest a trip to Mexico, sir. A face to face with President Rojo. He might like to hear his wife's final words."

Carter nodded again. "I think you're right. And Team Reaper should accompany us on the trip."

"A good idea, sir."

———

Presidential Palace, Mexico City

Kane hadn't counted on such a trip, but he didn't ignore the orders either. Neither did the rest of his team. They all had a score to settle.

Dressed for diplomacy instead of combat, Team Reaper carried only sidearms as they followed President Carter and General Jones into a private meeting room. They sat at a large table where glasses of water had been set out, but nobody took a drink, and nobody spoke. Kane looked at the wary faces of his teammates, the stern expressions of Carter and Jones.

Time to let the big men do the talking.

They had left Alamogordo behind three days earlier, with Sheriff Nazarian and his crew charged with cleaning up the mess at the cabin and dealing with the fallout. Federal agents in the area, sent by President Carter with explicit orders, were assisting with the clean-up. Cross and his militiamen would be left out of the eventual narrative which would leave Nazarian and his men the heroes of the day.

Nazarian hadn't been happy with the outcome, but also knew there was no room for argument.

President Rojo and his assistant, Federico Esteves, presently entered the room. They were not smiling.

Kane didn't blame them.

Rojo began with the usual pleasantries, shaking hands with President Carter. "I regret our meeting under these circumstances," Rojo said.

"We won't be long, Mister President," Carter said. He produced a smartphone from his jacket and tapped the screen. Placing the phone in front of where Rojo and Esteves sat, the group waited quietly as the words of Perlita Terrazas-Rojo, late First Lady of Mexico, filled the room.

Rojo sank in his chair as he listened. His face showed no emotion, his eyes glazed as he watched his wife's face and listened to the words coming out of her mouth.

She told everything. She mentioned names. Banderas and Zamorano. Rojo wondered where she'd learned the details. He hadn't kept the matter as quiet as he'd hoped. Surely somebody in his government had talked.

Esteves jerked his eyes around the room, freezing in his chair as his gaze landed on the hardened faces of Team Reaper.

The recording ended.

Carter picked up the smartphone and returned the device to his jacket.

"Here's the deal," the president said. "You might have concocted a nice cover story to explain why your wife was away at the retreat, but you'll have a hell of a time explaining why she's dead."

Rojo showed no reaction.

"You will reverse your policy," Carter continued. "You will tell us anything she left out, and we will allow you to bury her with dignity. After that, you will resign. Mexico will understand your grief. If you fail to do this, the whole story comes out."

Rojo looked across the table at Carter.

"What do you want to know?"

"The names of the people in the United States government that helped you."

Rojo quickly rattled off three names.

Stockwell.

Brinkley.

Ransom.

A fire began to burn in Kane's belly. He wanted those men's necks between his hands. They'd betrayed their country for money. Not for ideals, not for justice, but money. The worst kind of betrayal there was.

The meeting ended shortly after and the Americans left the palace to return to a waiting Air Force One.

On the flight home, the president outlined the next step in his plan.

To Kane, it was a sound plan.

———

El Paso, TX, Team Reaper Headquarters

Dr. Morales stopped the van.

Kane and his crew looked out the windows at the warehouse of their home. A fence surrounded the property, blocking most of the view, but the construction crew at the site was hard at work putting the building back together.

Later, at the Foundation Surgical Hospital, Kane and his crew visited each member of Team Bravo.

Kane sat beside General Mary Thurston as she lay in bed, telling her the entire story. He'd repeated the tale several times already, to the others.

When he finished, she shook her head.

"What happens now?" she said. Her voice was strong. She was doing very well, according to the doctor. They expected to release her and the other members of Team Bravo within a few days.

"We'll pay a visit to some people in D.C.," Kane said, "and finish the fight."

"Then what?"

"Then it's back to work, ma'am," Kane said. "HQ will be good as new, we'll have a chance to update our equipment, and we'll take on the next mission like none of this ever happened."

"But it did happen."

"And we've proven we're strong enough to overcome the obstacles, ma'am."

Thurston smiled. "Sometimes I wonder about you, Kane. One minute you've had enough, the next you're chomping at the bit to attack somebody."

Kane laughed quietly. "I'm full of surprises," he said.

"Get out of here," Thurston said. "You still have some work to do."

Kane rose from the chair. "Is that an order?"

"It is a direct order from your superior officer."

Kane smiled. It felt good to see her. It felt even better to see her, and the rest of Bravo, alive. "Yes, ma'am," he said.

West Coast of Mexico, Estate of Chucho Banderas

Victor Zamorano of the cartel bearing his name stepped out of the limousine and buttoned his coat as he surveyed the circular driveway and the amount of armed men stationed about. Movement on the roof caught his attention. That's where he saw a man with binoculars scanning the clear blue sky.

High alert indeed.

Chucho Banderas met Zamorano at the top of the steps between marble columns and they entered the mansion.

"What's happening, Chucho?" Banderas said as they crossed the tiled floor.

"I can't reach our people in America. I think they've run off."

"They won't be able to run far."

"Rojo is giving full power back to the military to come after us," Banderas said.

"They're already engaging south of Mexico City," Zamorano said. "I've lost several facilities already."

They stepped out on the rear balcony. More armed troops prowled the rear grounds.

"What's with the man on the roof?" Zamorano said.

"Looking for drones."

The pair sat at the same table as they had on their last visit and one of Banderas' servants brought sparkling water. Zamorano wasn't thirsty and let his glass sit on the table.

"I have a plane ready to take me to Nicaragua," Zamorano said. "From there I'll get to my hideout, but what about you?"

"Chopper's on the way. Same thing. By the time they catch up with us, we'll be long gone."

"Rojo is doing us a favor, you realize, by starting in the south."

"True. The Americans have him against a wall and we have him wedged in on either side. He has to give us time, or he knows we'll do worse damage to him than the Americans ever could."

"What about Stockwell and the other two?"

Banderas shook his head.

"You're sure?"

"Brinkley called me before being arrested. He says Team Reaper came after them. Stockwell tried to shoot first, and they blew him away. Ransom opted to take his own life; bullet through the head. Brinkley was going to shoot himself as well, but Reaper got to him first. He'll be dropped in a hole so deep he'll never see the sun again."

"So that's it then," Zamorano said. "We're on the run the rest of our lives."

Banderas laughed. He swallowed some of his drink. "But we'll still be in control of our various empires, Victor."

Men started shouting at the shriek of a jet motor drifting through the afternoon air. The man on the roof pointed, yelling, and automatic gunfire popped as troopers aimed at the sky.

Banderas and Zamorano jumped from their seats, looking up as a Predator drone zeroed in on the mansion in a steep dive. Zamorano screamed; Banderas laughed. Another rocket motor shrieked, the shockwave shaking the balcony as a contrail of smoke stretched from the roof to the drone. Seconds later, the drone exploded in a flash of fire.

Banderas clapped as Zamorano's shocked face turned his way.

"That's why I have men on the roof, Victor. You have to get up pretty early—".

Whatever Banderas was going to say never left his mouth. Another drone rocket, fired from far above, at a much greater distance than the decoy drone had flown, smacked into the center of the balcony almost directly behind the two men and obliterated them in an explosion so intense it toppled two nearby trees.

The echo of the blast carried through the air.

A LOOK AT: DANGER CLOSE (TEAM REAPER 12)
BY BRENT TOWNS

TEAM REAPER GOES GLOBAL

Reaper arrives in hell zone Afghanistan set on bringing justice to a Taliban opium warlord. Teamed with the CIA, Reaper wages a dirty war against international narco-terror and the casualties quickly pile up. In a single instant, everything unravels and the Team is decimated, forcing John Kane to continue the mission with a quick-on-the-trigger female intel officer wielding an extremely bad attitude and too many secrets.

Working with the Agency is never clean. Pursuing the target into Iran, Kane enters an espionage wilderness of mirrors; dealing with double-agents, unscrupulous mercenaries, and dubious government authorization. Following the bloody trail of an American traitor, Kane leads an assault on a horrifyingly well-defended Albanian island fortress.

The final firefight takes Reaper deep into the terror of combat and threatens to drown the Team in blood.

AVAILABLE JUNE 2025

ABOUT THE AUTHOR

A twenty-five year veteran of radio and television broadcasting, **Brian Drake** has spent his career in San Francisco where he's filled writing, producing, and reporting duties with stations such as KPIX-TV, KCBS, KQED, among many others.

Brian Drake lives in California with his wife and two cats, and when he's not writing he is usually blasting along the back roads in his Corvette with his wife telling him not to drive so fast, but the engine is so loud he usually can't hear her.

https://wolfpackpublishing.com/brian-drake/